I0599798

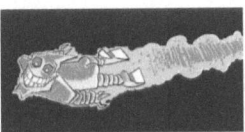

This is a work of fiction. Names, characters, places, and incidents either are the product of the author's imagination or are used fictitiously. Any resemblance to actual persons, living or dead, events, or locales is entirely coincidental.

Copyright © 2025 by Jorin Garguilo
ISBN 979-8-9924302-0-2 (paperback) ISBN 979-8-9924302-1-9 (ebook)

All rights reserved. Published in the United States by
FW Snaketiger Publishing.

LUNACY

A MAXIMALIST NIGHTMARE

JORIN GARGUILO

For mwh; I love you and you're directly responsible for a lot of the best stuff in my life

1

A wolf howled.

Nearby, Cheblenkov looked to the horizon, where day and night negotiated their transition through a smear of orange. It was time.

He walked behind the circle of small worn stones, away from the overlook, and sat down on a log bracketing the path. Resting his hands on his knees, he breathed deeply and slowly, staring to the distance.

As the moon came into view, Cheblenkov lifted his eyes toward it, head tilting upward. Then, in the pale light, he curled inward, dragging off each of his boots, spreading his hands across his knees, and sucking in a breath as his feet began to stretch painfully under the effect of the lunar rays.

THE FIVE WEREWOLVES stood within the stone circle, spaced apart at the five points of an invisible pentagram, moon suspended directly overhead.

They masturbated furiously.

Cheblenkov squeezed his ass cheeks together; his legs locked, his pelvis forward, his back arching.

Romana's arm was cocked at an angle as it jumped across her body vigorously.

Erskine kept his lupine eyes focused at the center of the circle, legs spread in a wide V.

Morduar handled himself slowly, like he was being played at quarter speed compared to his compatriots.

And Dennison kept looking around the circle, changing his stance and technique, and trying to make eye contact–unsuccessfully–with each of the pack.

The werewolves began to orgasm.

Morduar was first, ejecting a high-arching, long, lazy rope into the heart of the circle. Cheblenkov almost immediately added his spray, followed by a driving surge from Erskine. Romana squirted a volume accompanied by the hint of a rolling mist.

Several palpable moments later–and accompanied by a hint of dismay from the werewolves that had already made their contribution and creeping panic from the one that hadn't–Dennison finally flung his seed into the circle, stumbling backward and sheepishly glancing at his adjacent companions.

The werewolves then settled into their places around the perimeter and lifted their muzzles, emitting howls that blended together in the night air, floating upward to the moon.

In front of them, the ejaculate began to shift in its pool, flattening and flowing, deepening to a buttery color and swirling into a perfect circle. Defiant of normal geometry or physics, it began to rise, abandoning the flat plane of the ground, the circle becoming a sphere as it burst into the three dimensional space of the air.

This miniature twin to the moon rose up, spinning on its vertical axis.

Then it looked down onto the five werewolves encircling it, a smile breaking across the giant moon head. As the eyes of the buttery sphere blinked, a body in a gunmetal gray suit formed below. The moon man produced a matching fedora from nowhere and popped the chapeau onto its head. Jauntily, the moon man began a shuffling dance, vaguely recollecting Sherman Helmsley's side-to-side steps from that turn-of-the-century classic, *Amen*.

The werewolves howled.

Oh great, knives.

Lazy Nations had that one thought as she looked at the crowd outside the dingy convenience store.

Two little idiots had gotten in a shouting match that turned into a shoving match that now featured a couple of drawn blades in front of their friends. It looked like it wasn't going to be pleasant, and there were definitely people around that were not on board.

Looked like she was going to have to kick some ass.

Lazy Nations was the middle child of a man named Beautific Nations. She had one older sister, Crazy, and one younger brother, Gnarly.

"When you get a name like mine hung on you, you boil yourself alive figuring out if you're living up to it," her father had said. "Or, you just run the fuck away from it and never try. I didn't want to put that on my kids, so I went the other way with it. None of my kids is going to live up to their name. You're welcome."

Beautific Nations was for the most part correct in his assessment. And, he was a really solid single father.

Lazy Nations was not a particularly driven child, really, but she was absolutely not a shiftless one. If something needed to be done, she just did it, with zero compunction. There wasn't any particular eagerness to anything, or swiftness either, but no hesitation or equivocation. Just a paced, inexorable force dealing with whatever may have dropped in front of her.

She learned to fight with that same grinding, unrelenting way of moving. Beautific Nations neither condoned nor frowned upon what became Lazy Nations' daily ritual. She'd wake up hours before the sun, leave the apartment, and take the bus to whatever dojo or gym was the day's destination.

"I appreciate the drive, and your room isn't disgusting," is about all the editorial he had on the matter.

The evenness with which Lazy Nations conducted herself belied how good she was at fighting. She had a solidity to her, and a preternatural calm, and although not particularly fast, she was unerring in her targeting and extraordinarily powerful in contact.

She didn't even really have strong feelings about fighting, or feelings that led in some kind of abstract way to fighting. It was simply something she did, and she found herself in plenty of situations where it seemed like the most direct tactic to resolve the situation and keep moving forward.

~

"I WOULD LIKE to buy this can of beans," Lazy Nations said to the store clerk, "And also leave my backpack here for a moment. I'll be back to do some more shopping soon, and to retrieve my backpack."

The clerk nodded, most of his attention on the scrum coalescing immediately outside the door of the store. He had been working there for nearly six months and so far had stayed mostly unmolested, but the level of stress he felt for things that went on outside the front window was through the roof. He had seen some pretty strange and unsettling, if not outright scary, stuff.

Lazy Nations pushed out of the front door, the can of beans held casually in her left hand.

The two young combatants stabbed the air in front of them, leaping forward and back, snarling and threatening one another as the surrounding crowd cheered them on. The would-be fighters were nearly enclosed in the ring of onlookers, except for the side abutting the store's door.

"Hey, you're going to fucking hurt somebody, bad," Lazy Nations declared simply.

Each of the knife-wielders turned slightly toward her, both of them angry, if also a little confused at the interruption.

"So, I'm going to fuck you up," she continued.

The can of beans whizzed out of her hand and connected with the sternum of the assailant to her left. He wheezed as his chest compressed inward and his arms and legs flew forward, his body lifting slightly off the sidewalk. He dropped his knife.

Turning matter-of-factly, Lazy Nations then slapped outward against the knife arm of the other combatant, his weapon flinging itself upward and into the awning of the convenience store. Finally, Lazy Nations reached back, grabbing the collar and waist of her first target. Harnessing the rebound momentum as he stumbled back into the fight, she drove him forward, using his skull to absolutely flatten the balls of his opponent against his own body.

Dropping her human battering ram to the sidewalk, Lazy Nations turned away from the two groaning figures, each puffing hard and lying prone as she moved to reenter the store.

"I don't think you should be trying to kill each other anyway, but what you were up to was dangerous," she commented, more to the crowd than to the flattened figures. "There are people around here, you could hurt somebody."

The two were still stretched out, moaning but awake, and attempting to gather themselves when she exited the store again ten minutes later, her backpack holding the several items she planned to use to cook dinner for herself and her father that night.

3

The indoor garden was hot. Hot and exotic.

Dr. Martina Desmond moved down a row overhung with the tendrils of looming flora, swarming with the smell of earth and greenery.

"Wyatt, what's the reading on the L-1501?" the doctor asked. She angled around a large purple and green plant until she could see her assistant a few rows over.

"It's still weird. Very weird, really," replied Wyatt, setting down a tablet and pushing back his sweaty hair. "There's a lot of...pulsating?... pulsating stuff going on here. This level of cycling shouldn't be so obvious, I mean, I think I can *see* it...visually. Visually see it. Which seems way too over the top, even with the splices we put in there. They were adventurous splices, but..."

"All right, all right," the doctor interrupted, tapping her nails against her jawbone. "This specimen is bound to be, how you said it, a weird one–we're using animal blood to supplement and encourage the growth and bloom. Let's just observe it and see what we see, even if it's outside the bounds of expectation."

"Sure, sure, sure...of course, doctor," Wyatt replied. "But still, this feels pretty wild. I...I have this feeling watching it, I feel disturbed...but also like I want to dance?"

"Okay, Wyatt," said the doctor. "Let's stay disturbed. But also, we can dance a little. Let's dance a little."

Dr. Desmond pulled her phone out of her jacket pocket and swiped through a few screens of apps before tapping into one, swiping and tapping again.

A throbbing beat splashed across the garden, and the doctor began to bob up and down.

"The plants love it too, right?" the doctor asked, as she swayed from side to side and dipped on the beat.

"Right, yeah," Wyatt confirmed, beginning to gyrate across the rows himself. "They love it."

The plants, and L-1501 in particular, did love the music, and pulsated harder, rippling in the heat and music.

4

Zappazmazoid the robolien stood on the far side of the moon, watching space tilt before it.

Its sensors were so advanced it could, essentially, *feel*. It felt with an accuracy beyond the limits of the animal or human, although certainly the sensations transmitted were at a different admixture than the fleshy comparative.

And what Zappazmazoid noticed beneath its great, wide, metal feet was a disturbing deadness.

The damned spirit that had long raged under the lunar surface, and to which Zappazmazoid had become accustomed, was, quite suddenly, absent. Somehow, it had escaped its prison.

And Zappazmazoid was troubled by this. The robolien had been charged with keeping sentry against the vile spirit held within the crust of the satellite, and now the spirit had broken free, journeying across the slim void of space between the moon and the moon's near neighbor.

The robolien discharged an exhalation of a sort, venting an internal gas from its rotors into the void of space, watching the moisture within it crystallize. No longer engaged strictly in monitoring, Zappazmazoid would have to take action and pursue.

Combustion rumbled within the frame of the robolien, and it launched into space, curving in an orbit around the moon to align with the earth below it.

It blazed forward through the trash encircling the blue-green globe.

A satellite pinged off its angular shoulder, splintering and spinning in fragments into the space beyond. A teen's download was interrupted. The long pause in an awkward conversation became longer, more awkward, and ended with each side simultaneously asking "are you still there?" with no audible answer from either.

5

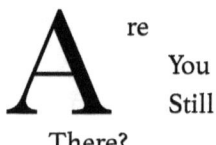

Are You Still There?

6

"That was pretty damn good," Beautific Nations commented as he rolled his fork over a couple of times in the remnants of the pasta sauce. "Who would have thought? Convenience store pasta and my girl makes it feel like something special."

A moment. Not an awkward one, but a moment passed.

"Well, me, I would have thought that," said Beautific.

"Not a surprise to me," Beautific added.

"So, how many asses did you beat on the way here?" Beautific asked.

"A couple," Lazy Nations replied.

From his tattered green and yellow plaid armchair, Beautific Nations assessed his daughter. "You know, I *could* wonder how the opposite of Lazy ended up being 'ferocious non-stop ass kicker'...but I guess it's a fool's errand to predict the full sum of the future. I love you, I'm glad for you."

"In a less violent update, how is this going?" he asked, gesturing to his emptied plate.

"Yeah, it's going well. I'm going to start at a kitchen

soon," Lazy Nations responded. "It's in a hotel, so that's... eh...but the reputation is not so bad. I think it will be good. And, you know, I don't mind work. Not at all. I sort of love work."

"OK, good. Good," Beautific Nations considered. "I love you. I think, sometimes, I tried so hard not to hang something on you kids, I really hung something else on you."

The old man drank in the air deeply. "How devastatingly Greek. I'm like Oedipus Dad or something. Tried to avoid fate so hard it snapped us all up."

He raised a beer to his daughter. "I'm just trying to say, you could give yourself a break sometime. It's something you could have."

7

T he lock took a bit of work. And then the deadbolt–
the deadbolt was equally fumbled, if not moreso.
When all of that was finally resolved, the knob
presented a final, additional challenge, jamming a few times
before the door finally swung open and Shelly Weedler
stood in the entryway to her apartment, a grimace on her
face.

"Yugh, it is really pungent out there. It's that gross place
across the street," she said, shutting the door behind her.

Her disinterested roommate, Gloria, shifted her head
very slightly and grunted, an acknowledgement that also
suggested she wasn't interested in whatever conversation
Shelly was trying to broach.

"Yeah, it's way earthy but kind of sweet. Sweet like barf
or something," Shelly continued as she stepped further into
the apartment, dropping each of her bags, and approaching
the window that faced the street. "It's very gross. And I hate
it. Yuck."

Gloria slowly moved her head back in the direction of
their television, casually enough as to indicate she didn't

want to have any engagement at all with the theoretical conversation.

"I don't know what's going on over there, I hope it's not a food thing, because, wow, I would not be hungry ever again if it was a food thing."

Gloria continued watching television.

"Because that is a very difficult odor. And it fills up the whole street out there, when it's bad."

Shelly put a hand on her hip and the other on the window frame. "Oh, get a load of this. This looks nuts. The parking gate is up from that place, and what is this guy doing? Driving some kind of giant plant out of there? He's got it belted into the passenger seat. And he's talking to it? Or himself? Too weird."

Gloria didn't move.

"OK, yeah. I'm going to put this stuff away," Shelly said, turning away from the window and returning to her bags.

"You're going out tonight, right?"

"Right?"

"Gloria, you're going out tonight?"

"Gloria."

"You're going out tonight?"

"Mm?" asked Gloria.

A moment of silence hung between the roommates.

"Yeah," Gloria intoned, absently.

8

"Heh, heh, heh," the wiry, goggle-eyed stranger chuckled, sidling up to the diner's counter.

The waitress behind it made a conscious decision not to ask what made the man so pleased with himself.

It didn't matter.

"Me and my friends," he said, issuing the invitation again.

She ignored it.

"Me and my friends," he chortled, "We just got up to something."

"What can I get you?" the waitress asked.

The nearly skeletal man glowered at the dismissal. "Coffee. Eggs, scrambled. Ham on the bone, right. It's on the sign."

The waitress nodded as she scribbled the order on a ticket and pinned it up behind her for the short order cook to fulfill.

The man pressed on though, despite the air of unwelcome. "Me and my friends, we got up to something. Something big. We made something."

"Nobody wants to HEAR it, you NUMB NUTS," an elderly man snapped from down the counter.

"Don't–" the thin man began, first pointing, then curling his hand into itself.

"Don't–" he tried again, unable to finish the sentence. Unable to phrase his warning to his fellow customer, obviously a regular at the diner. He didn't know what the old man shouldn't do, but he wasn't a fan of whatever this was.

"NUMB. NUTS," expectorated the man from his seat.

The waitress interceded dispassionately. "Here's that coffee. Eggs and ham on the way. You should probably settle down and be a little quiet. Wade over there. He's crusty. But. He's not really wrong. This isn't a place to be telling your private secrets."

Dennison scowled and clutched his coffee mug with two hands.

He and his friends had made something.

And he was going to smell Wade before he left the diner.

And then he was going to go to Wade's house the next time the moon was full.

And Dennison was going to eat Wade's ass right off his butt.

The next time the moon was full.

9

The Royal Leisure Motor Inn wasn't anything remotely approaching royal, and it would be incredibly difficult to feel comfortable enough to relax into a state of leisure there. Additionally, the idea of driving a motor vehicle up to it was an iffy proposition given the quality of the surrounding streets.

Even so, Wyatt pulled his car up to the curb near the motor inn's small office. He slid out of the driver's seat, strode across the sidewalk, and stepped into the cramped lobby.

The woman behind the counter eyed him suspiciously, adjusting her tropical-print polyester shirt as the sweaty young man approached and spoke in a jagged, conspiratorial tone.

"Vacancy?" he asked.

Before Marcy Egg could reply, he continued, "I need something with a couple of beds. Twins. Twins would be fine. And I want to be able to control the air myself. I want to be able to turn it off."

Marcy pointed her skepticism at him. "We don't want anything weird."

The pause hung in the air between them, and then Wyatt gave a single sharp nod. "But I can turn the air off. Two twins?"

Marcy sighed. After the recent outbreak that the locals were calling the Savage Rash was attributed to the motor inn, her boss had been on her ass about the prodigious volume of vacancy. Any patron was a welcome patron, even if they were a little off. Or a lot–everybody that visited the Royal Leisure Motor Inn was necessarily a little off.

"Air is on a unit right next to the door. Not going to be on unless you turn it on. Rooms are pretty hot. And kinda stale. We can't be wasting air, we're not a millionaire here. So you gotta turn it on. If you don't turn it on, it's just going to be whatever it is in there already."

Wyatt blinked.

"Oh, and all we got are queens," Marcy continued. "But we can roll one of the cots in there. We got three cots. No, two cots. A baby pooed on one of them and the state says we can't use it any more, but we still have it in the back office. Nobody knows what to do with that thing."

Marcy shifted when she realized what she had disclosed. Probably not the kind of thing to say to a customer. But this customer at least seemed unaffected.

She assumed that meant he was straying. "Welp. That's sixty-five for the night. With a five dollar key deposit on top. You get your five bucks back when you return the key."

Wyatt dug into his pocket and produced a card.

"We can do the card for the sixty-five, but the deposit has to be cash. ATM over there if you need it."

Wyatt swung his head around to the ATM behind him, hiding next to the door. He turned with his card toward it.

"So you know, there's a service fee on that thing."

Wyatt turned one sidelong eye back toward Marcy.

"Eight bucks," she said apologetically. "Or, eight fifty. I think."

Marcy thought she saw Wyatt wince, briefly.

But maybe it was a trick of her eyes.

"Visual on the Bogey," Captain Rick Hart reported as his jet cut through the clouds.

Hart's F-600 Bloodshrike held its position, slowing so that it hovered above the streaking shape, and pointing slightly down toward the unidentified object, striking a picture of predatory stillness, as though the jet hung in the air.

"Haven't seen anything like it before, but it is definitely a manufactured object," Hart said. "Not a meteorite."

The Bloodshrike banked and rotated to keep an intercept path.

"Not detritus either, it's moving under its own propulsion."

The Bloodshrike swooped to follow its target, keeping the gleaming metal entity lined up before it.

"You should have a feed, it is moving with intent ... permission to bring it down. Over."

"Permission granted, Captain Hart," the voice in his flight helmet confirmed.

Hart toggled the safety off of the Bloodshrike's throttle

and lined the target up on his quarry. He thumbed the switch twice, and a keening launch screamed through the air in the echoed pursuit of two Crimson Impaler missiles.

The first projectile hit and the object exploded on the contact. The second projectile tore the already shattered body into smaller fragments.

"Heading back to the homestead, over," said Captain Hart perfunctorily as the Bloodshrike blazed through the halo of tumbling debris.

Behind him, Zappazmazoid's squat head tumbled down through the sky, scorched, its nub sparking, but otherwise whole.

11

"Bye dad, have a good night," Lazy Nations said over her shoulder as she stepped out of Beautific Nations' apartment.

Across the hallway a door stood open, and Beautific Nations' neighbor teetered slightly in the frame. His mouth hung slack; his eyes stared through Lazy Nations in the vague direction of her father's home–but perhaps more accurately, he stared to a distance far beyond that which eyes could possibly reach.

"Uh..." Lazy Nations began.

"Quorbin. Quorbin!" her father said, stepping up to join her in the doorway. "Quorbin. You gotta go to bed. You're exhausted, man. You're out in the hall, standing up."

Matthew Quorbin stared.

When there came no answer, Beautific Nations stepped between his daughter and the dazed individual, holding out a hand to gesture from one to the other. "Well, Matt Quorbin, this is my daughter, Lazy. Lazy, this is Matt Quorbin, my neighbor. He's all right. He just doesn't get nearly enough sleep, so most of our conversations go about like this."

Matthew Quorbin seemed to nod in acknowledgement, or at least, Lazy and Beautific could have debated whether he had or not if they'd wanted, and neither would have been able to say for sure one way or another. Then, he stepped backward through the door into the dark of his apartment, and the door swung closed without any indication he had actually physically interacted with it.

NUDE, Matthew Quorbin stood in the dark of his small kitchen, the sole light in his home coming from the open microwave mounted above the oven.

Within, a porcelain bowl of milk sat with an entire stick of butter in it. The stick angled upward, breaking the surface of the liquid and just barely resting on the lip of the bowl.

Matthew Quorbin pushed the door of the microwave closed and dragged his other hand down along the controls as if lazily petting a dog, once. The microwave buzzed on and began rotating the bowl on its circuit.

Matthew Quorbin stared into the milk as it began to bubble and the butter melted down and was subsumed. A smell of fullness rolled out of the mixture and clouded the kitchen. It stared back at him, a pupil-less eye. Against the hum of the radiating microwaves and the crunching grind and squeak of the rotating platter, Matthew Quorbin imagined hearing a distant tune beginning to play in accompaniment. A scronking, lurching saxophone sound, pulling up and against the ever-more urgent rhythm of the machine.

Ding.

Silence, like an exhalation into the kitchen. And darkness, the microwave's light snuffed out for the moment.

Matthew Quorbin popped the microwave door open again by punching the wide button below the control panel.

He encircled the bowl with his fingers, a thumb and forefinger bracing it on each side despite the heat burning the pads of his digits.

Matthew Quorbin raised the bowl the full length of his arms above his head, again bathed in light from the open microwave door, pausing in a kind of supplication to an invisible force.

And then he overturned the bowl, and the burning dairy potion slid across his body.

Matthew Quorbin did not scream–he made no noise at all–as each of his orifices and protuberances slid easily off his body with the bath of liquid.

Every hair on his body, his eyes, his ears, his mouth, his nose, his nipples, his navel, his penis, and his butthole all washed off without resistance and rode the yellow-white wave to settle around him in a wet mess on the kitchen floor.

Quorbin stood, smooth and featureless.

12

S helly Weedler crossed the living room of the apartment, eating a bowl of cereal as she went.

Out of habit, she idled at the window overlooking the street outside. The television was on, turned low in the background, but as was so often the case, it was the window that drew her focus. Even when there was nothing to see, it was still where Shelly always returned when she found herself aimlessly pacing around the house.

As it turned out, tonight there was a bit more to see than usual.

A car pulled up and her roommate emerged from the back seat, returning home from an evening out.

"Gloria's home," Shelly said, scooping a spoonful of cereal into her mouth.

The taxi cab that had delivered Gloria drove away; just beyond, Shelly now spotted a woman in a lab coat appear at the end of the long driveway across the street. The woman heaved up the parking gate with her shoulder and then stumbled out onto the sidewalk.

"Huh," Shelly murmured.

From her position at the window, Shelly squinted. The woman wore a pump on one foot, but the other foot was sheathed only in a frayed stocking.

"One shoe," Shelly observed, letting her spoon rest in her cereal bowl.

Out on the street, Gloria turned her head, also curious about the woman in the lab coat.

The woman, halfway bent over to catch her breath, glanced up sharply and then stood, waving both arms above her head to indicate that Gloria should back away.

Instead, Gloria took all the waving as an invitation and began to walk *toward* her.

"No, no," Shelly called from the apartment. "That means *get back. Get back.* Not *come here.*"

Shelly put the cereal bowl on the sill and started glancing around at neighboring surfaces for her phone. She kept one eye on the window, of course, and watched as the woman in the lab coat began to pump her hands even more vigorously outward.

Gloria responded by speeding her pace of approach.

Behind the parking gate, a rolling cloud of purple particulate coalesced.

Shelly had to do something–her phone! There it was on the side table! She grabbed it and jammed her fingers across the device. "she mens get bak," she typed quickly.

Gloria finally slowed, tilting her head quizzically as the woman in the lab coat threw herself onto the ground.

From the window, Shelly saw her roommate reflexively look down as the text found its mark. Gloria pulled her phone out of her clutch, scanned Shelly's message, and then looked up just as the purple cloud enveloped her. It lingered for a moment, the precise length of an inhale and an exhale.

Then the cloud dissipated, stretching into the open air and floating off in every direction of the night.

The woman in the lab coat sat up, completely disheveled.

Gloria stood frozen in place. And suddenly, without warning, something seemed to erupt in her chest as her arms and head went slack. Then Gloria's head exploded.

"Oh," said Shelly, "Oh. Oh, wooooow."

"You may want to brace yourself, Detective Bunson," the fresh-faced uniform suggested. "This one is pretty far out there."

Bunson's partner, Detective Mandel, appeared in the hallway behind the kid. "Come on in, our guy is in the bathroom."

Detective Bunson followed Mandel down the carpeted hall, noting the deeply plowed furrows at waist-level on either side. Like someone had dragged some kind of tined steel tool along each wall while advancing.

The two detectives stepped into the narrow, yellow-tiled bathroom. The body lay on its stomach, stretched away from the door, feet pointing toward the detectives. The hands of the victim were splayed out, one resting on the lip of the toilet, the other laying against the base of the bathtub.

"Yikes," Bunson said.

"Yeah," Mandel responded.

The butt of the victim was missing, devoured to the bone, but only that exact portion of the body. The work pants were untouched, right up to the point where they were shredded through in the back. The waistband was intact, with the torn remnants of a soft flannel shirt still tucked into it. The slightly rotund torso and everything above it remained unmolested, aside from the light damage sustained by being slammed to the tile floor.

"Something ate this guy's ass," Bunson stated plainly.

"Yeah, funny you say it that way..." Mandel murmured.

Bunson did not appear to have heard. "So what do we actually know?"

"His name is Wade Watterson, 73, retired machine shop guy,"

"Any witnesses?" asked Bunson. "Anybody else in the house when it happened?"

Mandel nodded. "He was playing cards with his sister out in that front room. Alberta Jarvis, 68. Then some kind giant dog, or bear, came crashing through the window. *And* the wall, actually, it's kind of nuts what this thing did to the place–"

Bunson frowned. "Where's the sister now?"

"She's pretty shaken up," Mandel said. "We've got her outside, so we can try talking to her again maybe when she catches a little bit more of a breath, right. So anyway, this thing comes crashing into the house, apparently, and starts going after Watterson, stalking him, like, but ignoring our girl. She's just sitting there, holding her cards, with her mouth wide open."

Bunson nodded slightly toward the assless corpse, and then returned to the hall.

Mandel joined him, gesturing toward the living room. "So Watterson makes a run from there. Hide out in the bathroom. Hunker down in the tub like it's a tornado or something, or maybe get out the little window up over the tub.

Although at his age and state of health that would have been something to see."

Bunson grunted with disapproval at the aside.

"Anyway, this thing pursues him down the hall, dings up the walls like it's trying to scare the guy even more. Weird behavior for an animal."

"Sure," Bunson acquiesced. "What else?"

"Well," Mandel considered. "I guess there's also this. Right up here, looks like Watterson tried to slam the door closed behind him, but then this thing *grabs* the door by the hinge and crushes it open. You can see the claw mark where it clearly wrapped a paw around here and squeezed the edge. Not a bashing thing."

Bunson was silent.

"Yeah, so that's why the neighborhood is cordoned off and we've got all the animal control officers out there. Including the ones that look like they're dressed in mattresses or whatever."

"Okay. So, this is pretty damn weird," Bunson measured out his assessment. "And even sort of funny if that's your style. But I get the impression you didn't really tell me the really funny part yet."

"Oh– oh yeah," Mandel said, shaking their head. "Mrs. Jarvis is, naturally, pretty shocked, but one of the things she did say was that this thing was *talking*. She swore it was talking to Watterson after it broke in and while it was chasing him down the hall."

"*Talking*?" Bunson frowned.

"Yeah," Mandel said. "She swore it kept saying over and over, 'I'm going to eat your ass.' Or, I guess, specifically, it was: 'I'm going to eat your ass, numb nuts.'"

"Well, damn," said Bunson. "If we've got a big talking

dog, I guess it's a big dog with some very clear opinions about things."

14

Dennison was orgiastically gleeful when, shortly after he and his compatriots had summoned Mr. Moon, he discovered that the full moon had become permanently available to him, no matter what was happening with the actual heavenly body.

It was no more difficult than opening his digital wallet on the phone and selecting a card. Double-click the invisible button inside himself, and the full moon was another tap away.

Dennison loved his phone. He got service through Real Buddies Mobile, and he felt they charged a fair price and always had pretty good trade-ins, and while the coverage could probably be better, he didn't talk much on it, so it never really bothered him. He always neatly tucked his phone into a zipped plastic bag and stored it in a rocky hole or in the bole of a tree before a transformation.

Reverting to his human form had become much easier as well. It always seemed appropriately timed, and he didn't even have to think about it, which would have been challenging in his lupine form. It was like an electric kettle clicking itself off once the water was boiling. Click, the water has boiled, the job is done, back to human form.

DENNISON ZIG-ZAGGED toward the blockade across the street. "Whoa, whoa, whoaaaaa...what happened here?" he asked the cop behind the obstacle.

"Ahhhh, sounds like something crazy," answered the patrolman. "Some kind of animal attack, some animal ate some old man's whole ass."

"GAVIN!" exclaimed a nearby officer. "We can't say stuff like that! People aren't supposed to know details like that."

"I'm sorry sir," the young man muttered.

The other officer stepped forward, taking charge. "There has been an incident that is as-yet unclear with respect to a resolution. This and surrounding streets are closed to through-traffic. If you are a resident, one of our officers will accompany you to your home, and we're asking all residents to shelter in place with doors and windows locked." The man looked expectantly at Dennison, apparently waiting to hear his residency status in terms of the neighborhood.

"Oh, yeah, uh, I guess I'm through-traffic," Dennison replied, contorting his neck to peer up the street. He twitched happily. "Guess I'll have to...go around."

"Very well, you have a good night sir, and be careful out there."

"But it is *true*," insisted Gavin quietly. "That animal ate some old man's ass right off his butt, I heard, down to the bones."

"It sure did," Dennison murmured with a satisfied smirk as he wandered away from the blockade.

Dennison hadn't moderated his volume, so the officers

certainly heard his comment, but it didn't register to either of them. Instead, the older officer glared at Gavin and began to scold him again.

15

Marcy Egg raised her eyes from the key on the desk of the Royal Leisure Motor Inn office. She reached into the cash drawer and drew out a massively crumbled five dollar bill that was somehow vaguely moist, and pushed it across the front counter.

"There's your deposit, hope you enjoyed your stay, come back and see us again," she said flatly.

In actuality, the keys were not terribly valuable. Behind the desk, there was a big sack filled with them, and, as it turned out, all of them were the same, and any one of them would open any of the rooms of the Royal Leisure Motor Inn. The idea that they had value was a facade that classed up the place a little–and often netted an extra five dollars in cash per guest.

"Ahhh, it was alright," the bald man replied. "I got a little sleep but this place is hot. Really stuffy."

Marcy looked at the guest without expression.

After a beat, she explained unconvincingly, "It's the highway, everything is hot around here, because, um, the heat gets into kind of a bowl and then empties down the service road, and then, we, uh, we get it. And so does the car place on the other side. It's even hotter there. With the cars."

"Well, yeah, that makes sense," he agreed, not really understanding the explanation, but not wanting to show that he didn't understand. "Yeah, OK."

As he turned to leave, the man noticed a little pile of comment cards off to the side of the desk, next to a couple of stubby pencils. He course-corrected toward them, dragging one of the cards over to the edge of the counter and then slanting himself diagonally away from Marcy to keep her from watching.

As if, she thought.

He picked up one of the short pencils and screwed up his mouth as his brow knitted together. The tip of his tongue poked out and one eye squeezed closed as he scrawled a couple of words, and then, after a pause, dashed off another several sentences quickly.

Without looking at Marcy, he nudged the card across the counter toward her, spun around, and then quickly exited the office. His pickup truck rolled past the window and Marcy watched it pass with disinterest. Then she slid the card closer and turned it over to read the uneven hand-writing:

TOO HOT.

Also, strange smell. Something growing against one wall. Water damage? Lived in a trailer for a while that got black mold. Kinda has that same feeling. Not that, but kind of feels like it. Call remediation service? Could be serious. Microwave very disgusting. Shower was dirty.

Marcy shrugged, tore the card in half and dropped it off the side of the desk. Each half just missed the trash can, fluttering to the floor.

16

A whine somewhere in the distance brought Carol out onto the porch. She searched the sky for the source, as the sound grew louder and Biscuit, her chocolate lab, did laps around her legs.

From inside the house, Amy started to ask a question about dinner.

"Wait, wait, shh," Carol shushed her. "Do you hear that? Seems like it's getting louder–is there a plane or something doing something weird?"

Amy joined Carol on the porch, tilting her head to try to catch the sound.

"Oooh...yep, yep, I think I hear it," Amy confirmed. "Kind of like a racecar sound, without the engine part, like, though."

Biscuit stopped circling, pointed his muzzle up toward the sound, and began to whine in harmony.

The volume of the sound rose to an ear-splitting level and then suddenly, it was completely surrounding them. At which point the source of the noise arrived with a scream–

and the utility shed in the backyard exploded in a burst of flames.

"Ahhhhhh!!!!!!" screamed Amy.

"Oh shiii—-" yelled Carol.

Biscuit barked and tore off from the back porch toward the ruined shed.

"*Biscuit!*" Carol called, stumbling down the path after him. Behind her, Amy's knees gave way and she sank onto the outdoor couch.

The dog disappeared into the intense cloud of dust encircling what was once a perfectly nice place to keep gardening supplies.

"*Biscuit!!!*" Carol pleaded again.

"Be careful," Amy called weakly from the porch.

Carol glanced back over her shoulder, hesitating, and then took several steps closer to the wreckage. She blinked against the settling dust as the silhouette of...something... began moving toward her with a slow lurching gait.

"What is...Biscuit?" The words fell from Carol's lips in utter bafflement.

On the porch, Amy blinked, squeaked, and fainted.

But it *was* Biscuit, more or less. He stepped forward on his hind legs, his forelegs dangling like arms. His tongue hung from his mouth, and the dog seemed happy enough.

On top of the dog's head, another head sat, this one made of metal. The rough features of a human face were cut into its alien alloys, and a reverberating buzz of static resolved itself into echoing words from the additional head.

"The dog and I have come to an agreement," it said. "I have need of a body to complete a very important task, and he has agreed to lend me his for the time being. He will be compensated through a rewarding chemical process and I

will guarantee, to the best of my prodigious calculatory ability, his safety over the course of this union."

Carol's knees buckled slightly as her body made an
argument to join Amy in her approach to the situation.

17

E lvin and Darcy were a well-oiled machine behind the counter of the Maximum Burrito.

Sometimes, when walking into another Maximum Burrito, one could encounter three or four or five or even six employees behind a counter, and the whole process could involve a lot of waiting and miscommunication and disinterested standing around by some portion of said staff.

Not the case with Elvin and Darcy at Maximum Burrito number one five four, 2407 Chestnut Avenue.

They put on an impressive dance, weaving back and forth so that no space was wasted, and even if a customer equivocated or had questions, it just fell into the tapestry of the rhythm of the ever-pulsing burrito machine.

Elvin or Darcy would initiate the order, sometimes down the line far enough it could surprise a patron, and then each would contribute to applying ingredients, applying *other* ingredients, rolling, wrapping, bagging, or transacting the payment process.

And they'd seen some pretty weird stuff, dealt with some

pretty weird people, and taken some pretty strange orders, never wavering in their exquisite competence since finding one another.

It was a sight to behold, but also so smooth and modest, most people didn't even notice it.

18

Do you need a buddy?
Do you have some buddies?
And allyouneedtodo
Is getintouchwiththem
We can help you with that!
Reaaaaaal
Budddddddies
Mo-
Bile!

19

S helly Weedler cracked open the front door of the apartment building and looked out onto the street. Almost no hint of the purple cloud remained, aside from a stray floater here or there, although the air itself had a hot heaviness, noticeable even through the mask Shelly had pulled on out of an abundance of caution.

Across the street Dr. Desmond slowly made her way to the sidewalk, shaking her head as she reached Gloria's remains.

Shelly hesitated at the doorway, then abruptly stuck her arm outside, waving to catch Dr. Desmond's eye. The doctor noticed and limped over as quickly as she could, slipping inside the mailroom as Shelly stepped back to admit her. The door slammed shut behind them, and the doctor leaned back against the wall before sliding down to sit on the foyer floor.

Shelly stared at the woman in the lab coat.

"What..." Shelly began, "...*the fuck*?"

Dr. Desmond closed her eyes. "Did you...how much did you...did you see that?"

"*That* was my roommate," Shelly said. "Gloria. Yes. Yes, I saw *that*. What was that? What was…"

The doctor rubbed her head.

"I should call somebody." Shelly pulled her phone out of her pocket. "I've called 411 about your place before and they didn't do anything but this is definitely a 911 situation or maybe I should call Gloria's family but I don't know any of them we didn't really talk about them we were roommates but it's not like we were close."

Shelly looked down at Dr. Desmond expectantly.

The doctor kept her eyes closed. "Yes. You should call someone. Start with 911 and we can see where it goes from there. Make sure you mention that there is a biohazard involved so they send the correct services."

"Biohazard?"

"Yes. Biohazard. Also, I need to get myself checked out. I imagine I've been building a slow resistance by working in the environment over the last several months, which is why my reaction to the biocloud was not as…violent…as your roommate's, but there could be more complications and consequences as a result of that."

"Uh huh," Shelly agreed. "Oh. Wait, so are we all in trouble? Everybody on the street? From the stink? What is that, by the way? That's why I've been calling 411, your place stinks."

"Yes, the odor can be powerful," answered the doctor a little too calmly. "But in general, simply smelling it at the remove of the street oughtn't be a concern. The material at that level of dissipation isn't enough to manifest a physical effect, you have to experience it at a higher concentration at a greater proximity."

Doctor Desmond finally opened her eyes. She surveyed Shelly. "You're fine."

Shelly let go of a breath.

"It only came to this because my assistant–and I didn't know it until I just arrived at the garden– my assistant removed the queen unit. It had been regulating the entirety of the garden, and without it, the other subjects cycled to the point of predatory physicality and then superemission. I don't know why he did that or where he is or what it is now in this state."

Shelly waited to hear more.

"That must be difficult to follow," admitted Dr. Desmond. "Our garden here is an incubator for experimentally splicing animal characteristics into vegetative matter. Our goal, while ambitious, is to create the equivalent, well, the actual manifestation, of warm-blooded plants. Plants that can self-regulate so that they may grow in any kind of weather with a minimal amount of tending. Imagine an orange grove on the tundra. Crops that shrug off blight, heat, or flooding. We're years away from that, but we were starting to see some results.

"Some...very interesting results." Dr. Desmond stared up to the ceiling of the foyer. "The recent changes came on so rapidly. It had all seemed theoretical and increasingly unlikely. Then things...just started to happen. To work? I don't know if that's the best way to say it. It sounds horrible right now. The queen emerged, the whole garden responded, we started observing things in the last few days and weeks that we hadn't seen in over a year, and we have no idea why. There wasn't any significant change in our methodology."

Dr. Desmond glanced back at Shelly with a shrug. "Everything just came to life after the last full moon. I remember coming into the garden and looking up and seeing it, then walking in and noticing the queen responding beyond anything since the start."

"Okay," Shelly replied. "I'm calling 911."

J oe Hickock had been hiking the mountain for the better part of the day. It'd been nice and the air was crisp, which felt especially pleasant as he'd surmounted some of the steeper inclines.

It was just about time for a break when he discovered a path tucked into the trees. He followed it, ambling along as it gradually sloped out to a secluded vista that curved away against the mountainside.

As he reached the clearing, he noticed the stones that had been precisely and intentionally arranged, worn down as they were to barely remarkable nubs. One of the stones was subtly different in color and substance than the other four, and seemed to give off a faint, luminescent glow.

But more striking than that was the perfect circle of black that sat in the center of the stones.

Had someone come out here to lay a perfect circle of asphalt? On top of a mountain? Why? How strange.

Mesmerized, Joe stumbled forward into the ring.

As he stepped inside, he was immediately overwhelmed by the sensation that his body was not so much encased as it was intermixed with some rock foreign to the earth. He hung in that nowhere place momentarily and then began to accelerate through it, a remote sense of crackling and popping to let him know he was being flung at a great speed, although the general feeling in his body was one of numbness.

Then, at the apex of his velocity, he slipped through the unbroken surface of the moon and was ejected into space.

Joe Hickock's body floated lazily into the inky darkness, rotating listlessly as it tumbled away and out into the void.

M andel tossed a stack of papers down on their desk. "Nothing, nothing yet. No dog, no bear, no giant psycho in a bear or dog costume."

Bunson slouched back in his chair, fingers steepled, and indicated for Mandel to continue.

"Mrs. Jarvis doesn't have any better recollection of what it was, and is now doubting what she initially reported about the dog talking. She thinks she might have imagined that after she saw what happened and maybe it was just growling weird because it was sick or something."

"Well, that probably doesn't get us further even if it doesn't get us closer," Bunson said with a sigh. "It's not like the animal control people can round up some animals and we can just see which one talks to us, and then say 'that's the one.'"

Mandel grimaced in agreement as they sat across from Bunson.

Bunson abruptly changed the subject. "Did you talk to Krenshaw and hear about that thing? Apparently there are these packs of people running around in morphsuits smashing stuff up and chasing after people. We haven't found any of them, but there have been about six or seven different calls about it just tonight. Just haven't put anybody in the back seat of a cruiser yet. Shit is going down tonight. Weeeeeird night."

"Wow." Mandel scratched their head. "Is there a full moon tonight, or what?"

B eautific Nations allowed his irritation to slow his pace as he crossed the apartment. "Okay, okay, all right–I said I'm coming."

The incessant knock was more of a rhythmic pounding, what sounded like two fists beating at the same time, high on the door.

"Lazy, if this is you, you have achieved a new level of annoying, and I already apologize for whatever I did to deserve it."

Beautific Nations swung the door open and blinked in surprise.

A tall, naked figure, absent any features or orifices, swayed in front of him, its fists raised midswing.

"Quorbin?"

The figure rushed in on him.

~

Lazy Nations exited the stairwell into the hallway of her father's apartment building. She pocketed her key and adjusted her backpack so it was more comfortable.

After having spent a few minutes at the bus stop on the corner, she was already returning, telling herself that it was simply because she'd meant to borrow her father's sewing machine, and had forgotten. Her jacket had been ripped when she knocked out a big guy for yelling at a family after a road rage incident (which was the big guy's fault), and he grabbed her jacket and didn't let go on his way to hitting the street.

Actually, she had a stack of clothes that needed little touch-ups here and there because different people had been a little handsy when she'd had to put them on the ground, and the jacket was a good excuse to knock through the whole pile.

But really, she also had a weird, bad feeling. And she'd developed a very good sense of the kind of weird and bad feelings that needed to be resolved by a fight. Her dad's neighbor struck her as a weirdo, and that wasn't a tough one to call, but as she got further away from the apartment the distant sense that he was also a bad-o crept up on her, closer and closer, an inverse of the number of steps she took away from her father's front door.

She didn't know why exactly, but she got the pretty confident sense that she was going to have to kick her dad's neighbor's ass tonight, and would probably have to put him down hard...maybe knock him out all the way and shove him in a closet and call the cops even.

"Dad?" Lazy Nations called out, far enough down the hall now to see the front door of her father's apartment yawning open. "Ah, shit."

Lazy Nations picked up her pace, although she didn't break into a run–running was a rarity for her. Nothing ever seemed that urgent, just inexorable.

So, inexorably, Lazy Nations stepped into the apartment. She dropped her backpack and swept her eyes across the place. It looked like a few things by the door had been jostled, and then something or somebody...her father, she presumed...had been dragged across the circular table in the dining area and into the main room with the television and the big window out onto the street.

She strode toward the main room, where she first clocked her father's armchair on its side and then the legs of the upturned coffee table. As she stepped into the archway of the room, she noticed the television, flickering with the images of the old detective show Scarecrow and Mrs. King. And in front of it, of course, the ongoing struggle.

Lazy Nations met Beautific Nations's gaze. His eyes bugged out toward her, desperate, as he scrabbled at the mildew-colored hands clasped around his neck.

"LAZY," Beautific Nations mouthed with a choke.

She advanced, singular in purpose.

The Quorbin wheeled around as it sensed her approach, simultaneously–and effortlessly– tossing Beautific Nations to the side where he landed in a painful jumble against the skewed coffee table.

The Quorbin was fast and strong, but direct. There was no feinting or disguising its intention as it closed in on Lazy Nations.

She slanted her body sideways to avoid a telegraphed blow and then hammered a hard fist into the torso of her assailant.

Lazy Nations felt the tough shell of the Quorbin's thick skin beneath her knuckles, but her punch had landed force-fully enough that she could also sense a quality of softness beyond it. Sponginess almost.

The creature slammed into the wall, plaster falling from

the heavy dent it left–but it recovered quickly, pivoting to box Lazy Nations into the corner. She put one foot behind her to set her stance and rolled her fists.

Before she could strike, the Quorbin snatched both her arms, pinning them to her sides, and smashed her into the wall to her left and then to her right, using the living room corner to bludgeon her from each direction.

"Lazy!" gasped her father as he tried to pull himself up.

Lazy Nations, arms trapped, swiveled her gaze to her father, then back to the monster holding her. Suspended by its grasp, she drew her knees up to her chest, inhaled, and then kicked both feet out and through the chest of the Quorbin.

Her shoes burst through the rind facing her, through the soft interior of its torso, and again through the stretchy, resilient outer layer of its back.

The Quorbin froze, its grip tightening momentarily and then slackening as its soupy, tapioca-like interior poured out of the giant hole in its body. Lazy Nations continued her trajectory through the hole she'd created, taking the creature down as she went. Its insides spread across the floor, ruining the carpet.

She stepped out of her adversary's chest hole and turned to look with some pinched concern at her father. "Dad, are you alright? How hurt are you?"

Beautific Nations groaned and, leaning back to brace himself against the wreckage of the table, held up his hands reassuringly. "I'm fine, I'm fine."

Lazy Nations eyed him with suspicion, and then looked back at the corpse of the Quorbin as its sauce continued to leak out, the featureless casing rapidly flattening in the dancing light of the television.

"Whatever this is," she remarked, "I don't like it much."

23

C aptain Rick Hart changed from his flight suit to his uniform and then stepped into the briefing room midway along the sleek, black hall.

Already seated inside was another member of the Secret Rapid Defense Force, Captain Veronica Boner, and pacing in front of the wall-sized digital display was his commanding officer, General Emmanuel Bowser.

"Ah, Captain, great," Bowser said. "Have a seat, let's get started looking at this thing you tangled with up there." The general turned toward the display, his back to the seated pilots, and tapped through a few readouts on his tablet. "Here's the footage Captain Hart captured in his pursuit and encounter."

All three of them watched the video at half-speed as Bowser narrated. "It's behaving like a rocket, or a missile. Definitely not debris on an orbit decay trajectory."

"Unusual shape, though," Hart interjected. "Slowed down like that, easier to see that it doesn't have a form factor like any of the stuff we–or any of our hostiles–have in the cabinet."

"You don't know the half of it," Bowser agreed grimly. "Metallurgical reads have been processed; the alloys are unusual, and, as yet, aren't indexing to anything we've got in the big book. There's some speculation running around that they, and this thing, are not terrestrial."

"So then... *extra*... terrestrial...?" Captain Veronica Boner ventured.

Bowser coughed in understated affirmation. "Well, and, there's no particular reason to be cute about this," the general picked up again, swiping his fingers across the tablet.

The recording sped to the point where Captain Hart's missiles achieved impact, advanced just beyond, and then slowed to scant frames per second, zooming in to track the path of a specific fragment thrown from the explosion.

"Does that look like a..." Boner began.

"A face," confirmed Hart. "It's a face."

After a brief pause, Hart cleared his throat. "That thing I blew up had a head. With a face."

"Affirmative," Bowser continued. "And that face, that head, hit the surface, blew up somebody's shed, and per satellite reconnaissance remained intact enough to then..."

Bowser tapped again. "Attach itself to a dog."

A jerky video of a chocolate labrador retriever appeared, on which was stacked the head from the previous video; the dog standing on its hind legs, jerkily sauntering down a sidewalk. In the background, a plume of smoke lingered in the backyard of a home.

"To all appearances, we had an extraterrestrial presence intending to pay a visit to our planet. Despite Captain Hart's intercession, the visit was not prevented. And now it is out there walking around on a canine, we can only assume with a plan to complete whatever mission it originally meant to accomplish."

Captain Hart raised an eyebrow at the general.

The general nodded. "That is the mission. Saddle up, the both of you, and intercept this visitor. Retrieve it and return to the laboratory here."

Hart and Boner stood, saluted, and moved to the door before hearing Bowser behind them.

"Ah, and if we can help it, let's try not to hurt the dog, right?"

Captain Veronica Boner looked at the general with a disgusted expression.

Hart shook his head in agreement with Boner. "Obviously, sir. We're not going to hurt the dog."

24

Dennison's confidence was growing to unwieldy proportions.

Having experienced the satisfaction of parceling out what he perceived to be a totally deserved allotment of comeuppance to Wade Watterson, Dennison was beginning to move through his days and nights looking for reasons to feel affronted.

It was a bit like perusing a menu. What insignificant, minor insult from a hapless stranger might inspire the next hunt?

Dennison lingered on a bench across the street from a Maximum Burrito.

Neither of the individuals inside had actually slighted him in the least. They had taken his order, prepared a perfect burrito, and done it all at an amazingly efficient clip.

But it stuck in Dennison's craw that they were unshaken by any of his questions, his reversals of decisions, his awkward pacing, his insistence on being difficult about his payment method. They treated it all like it was nothing, handled it like it was nothing. Was he nothing? He really should have been notable. But he wasn't. They didn't seem to mind at all. Didn't seem to notice.

Dennison stretched his arms across the back of the bench and stuck out his long legs, keeping his eyes level through the window of the Maximum Burrito.

It had a nice ring to it: Massacre at Maximum Burrito.

25

M arcy Egg swept up trash in the courtyard parking lot of the Royal Leisure Motor Inn. It was something she was supposed to do twice a week, and she mostly stuck to that schedule.

The courtyard accumulated a lot of junk, either from patrons or passersby or just wind blowing it in off the street. Cans and wrappers and paper. Marcy busied herself collecting it into her industrial dustpan and emptying that into the bin she'd dragged out from the office.

She swept an empty bag of chips into the dustpan and stood, gazing toward the rooms that lined the courtyard. Marcy blinked a few times as she assessed the room on the deep right corner. Number six.

The windows were shuttered, as was the case with most of the rooms, but it looked like the outer wall of the motel had become discolored around the door of number six. It even seemed to creep to either side, beginning to extend tendrils across numbers five and seven.

"Whelp, I should probably check that out," reflected

Marcy. Then she looked down at her plastic wristwatch. "Buuuut...shift is almost over. I'll check it out tomorrow."

Marcy dragged the bin back into the office, slipped the broom and dustpan beside it, flipped the "Closed 4 Business" sign face out and the lights off, and locked the door.

The key to the office also matched the keys to all of the rooms, incidentally.

Marcy climbed into the driver's seat of her ancient purple two seater hatchback and rolled away from the Royal Leisure Motor Inn, watching it– and the door to number six– recede in the rearview mirror.

26

A pair of diners, having wrapped up their meals at the same time, converged on the exit of the Maximum Burrito and began the awkward dance of sorting out who would be first out of the restaurant. They each chuckled disingenuously after working it out, and proceeded to make a more orderly exit before spying the approaching customer through the glass of the door.

One man scrambled back out of the way, his legs a cartoon jumble of motion, as he dove into a booth and slid under the table to hide. The other hesitatingly opened and held the door, his jaw slack with surprise.

Zappazmazoid and Biscuit strolled into the Maximum Burrito, the dog's hind legs slightly bow-legged as it walked. As they passed the astonished diner holding the door open, Biscuit yipped politely and Zappazmazoid intoned, "Thank you for your hospitable assistance" in an electric tone bracketed on either side by a wiggle of static.

The patrons of the Maximum Burrito gasped and began chattering quietly to one another as Biscuit and Zappazmazoid approached the counter. The previous customer quickly finished paying for her burrito bowl and scrambled away from the register as the combination dog-and-robot stepped up.

Behind the counter, Elvin's eyes widened by the slightest margin. His hesitation may have been as long as the width of a sheet of paper, but that was all it was– between him and Darcy, Maximum Burrito one five four was a well-oiled machine.

"Welcome to Maximum Burrito, how can we take it to the max for you today?"

Biscuit panted hungrily as Zappazmazoid buzzed in answer, "My companion requires sustenance and enjoys when his human associates share meals from this location. I require brown rice and beef."

"Brown rice beef bowl," Elvin repeated, scooping a ladle of brown rice into a pressed cardboard bowl and handing it to Darcy on his left, who immediately tonged slivers of beef into it.

"I would like to double the portion of beef," Zappazmazoid amended the order.

Darcy flipped the tongs around the outer edge of her hand and regripped them, pulling off an impressively dexterous maneuver without any distracting flourish, and exactly doubled the portion of beef in the bowl. Behind her, Elvin crossed to a spot further down the counter and held out his right hand. "How else can we top this brown rice double beef bowl for you?" he asked.

Biscuit lurched down the counter line, the dog's tongue hanging hungrily from his mouth, eyes fixed on the bowl-in-preparation. Zappazzmazoid merely nodded in approval. "Beef and brown rice are sufficient. Other ingredients will make my companion defecate in an undesirable fashion."

Elvin swung the bowl back in Darcy's direction. In a

single, smooth motion, Darcy tonged a little extra beef into the bowl Elvin held out, returned the tong to its place of rest, and slid around her colleague to a spot behind the register, taking the bowl from him as she reached his far side.

"Brown rice double beef bowl, that's eight forty-three," Darcy prompted. "Eating in or taking it to go?"

"Eating in," Zappazmazoid replied, transmitting payment from his robot head to the point-of-sale device.

Darcy lowered the bowl to the counter as Elvin slid a tray underneath it, leaving it handily available to the dog-and-robot.

Biscuit's forepaws slid under the tray, and as one, the two of them turned toward the dining room.

A palpable hush fell over the gathered crowd as Biscuit and Zappazmazoid made their way, one paw-step at a time, to a table in the back corner.

"Thanks for your business!" Elvin called.

"We hope to see you again at the Maximum Burrito!" added Darcy.

27

Activity swarmed the street between the garden and Shelly Weedler's apartment building. A sheet covered Gloria where she had fallen, and emergency vehicles formed an outer ring, blocking the street entirely. Closer to the opposite side of the street, large dark vans formed an inner ring, walling off the small parking lot of the garden. Figures in heavy, ventilated suits could be glimpsed moving equipment and containers in and out of the parking lot.

"O-kaaaaaaaaay," Mandel began as they trotted up. "Apparently that is 'nothing at all' and 'not a police matter.'"

"So, let's talk about what you saw happen to your friend," Bunson continued, waving over his shoulder to where Gloria lay.

Shelly Weedler and Dr. Desmond stood shoulder-to-shoulder, each with a blanket draped over them. Shelly wasn't really sure why, once all these official people started showing up, one of them offered her a blanket, but it seemed nice, so she took it and had been standing under it just watching all the vehicles and people fill in the street.

The two plainclothes officers had shown up most recently, asked their names, and then circulated between all the collected groups on the street before returning to begin their line of questioning.

It didn't seem like their circuit resulted in them learning much of anything about what had transpired– and their attempt to question Shelly and the doctor was looking increasingly doubtful as a stern woman in a dark gray suit approached. She had a wide face seemingly built for radiating dispassionate disappointment, and as she neared, she lifted two fingers before popping then back toward herself.

"Dr. Desmond," she interrupted. "We need to have a discussion."

The doctor glanced between the faces of Bunson and Mandel with pinched concern and apology, and then nodded even more apologetically to Shelly. Then, without another word, she broke off and followed the woman in the dark gray suit away from the group and back toward the black vans.

"Hey!" Bunson called, taking a step in her direction. That was as far as he got, though, because Mandel quickly put a forearm across his chest and gave a sharp, curt shake of their head.

Bunson sighed, gritted his teeth, and turned back to Shelly. He glanced down at his notebook, and then made an effort to begin again. "Alright, so, what can you tell us, Ms. Weedler?"

Shelly looked at the two officers and screwed up her mouth, eyes looking up as she tried to pull out of her brain exactly what she could tell them. She didn't really understand much of it, to tell the truth, and she knew she was going to make absolutely no sense at all if she tried to relay what Dr. Desmond had communicated to her. And given the attention from the mysterious gathering here, maybe she wasn't even supposed to do that, even if it did seem completely unbelievable.

"I..." Shelly eased into giving it a shot.

Mandel stepped back and withdrew a phone from their pocket, putting it to their ear and peppering quiet affirmatives to the voice on the other end of the line.

Bunson shaded his eyes momentarily toward Mandel, then cleared his throat. "All right, let's start at the top. You saw this...biohazard thing...and it...did what got done to your roommate, Gloria Smern?"

Before Shelly could respond, Mandel placed a hand on Bunson's shoulder. "We've got to go."

"We *what*?" replied Bunson. 'We've barely gotten anything here."

"We've got to go," repeated Mandel. "A talking dog just ordered a burrito bowl at a Maximum Burrito over on Chestnut."

"Oh. Oh, shit," a stunned Bunson stammered.

The two officers sprinted to their car, flung themselves inside, and peeled out, burning rubber as they went.

Shelly Weedler stepped out into the middle of the road, blanket still wrapped around her shoulders, and watched their car recede in the distance as it fishtailed forward.

"Talking dog," she murmured blankly.

Behind her, three pale, featureless figures ran from one alley to another.

28

Lazy Nations ran her hand through her hair as she walked down the street. She was still really confused as to what, exactly, she had dispensed in her father's apartment. She didn't have an outsized amount of patience for the strange; she mostly just broke things down to whether something should be left alone, protected from harm, or interceded against. Everything else was just living, one step in front of the other. She thought she probably was going to have to call her sister or brother and get some help figuring it out – they were both a lot better about more experimental thinking in each of their ways– but she really couldn't sort out exactly what she might say to them in the first place.

Well, enough of that for now. One thing she did know was that she needed to get something to eat, and that, at least, was something small and simple.

~

BISCUIT HELD the cardboard bowl between his paws as he sat in the booth at the Maximum Burrito. He had eaten the entire meal, and was licking his tongue around the bowl to pick up the last few grains of rice. Zappazmazoid sat impassively atop Biscuit's head, waiting for his companion to finish.

The front door of the Maximum Burrito burst open, and Mandel rolled into the restaurant, landing in set position on their knees near the lip of the counter. They'd regret the roll later, in particular swabbing their nice dress shirt across the floor of a Maximum Burrito, but, for now, their training put that consideration out of their mind.

"Hold it right there– dog!" Mandel shouted, pointing their service weapon across the restaurant at Biscuit.

"Everybody keep calm," Bunson directed, sliding in to pin the door open and leveling his own weapon at Zappazmazoid and Biscuit. "We just need to ask the dog a few questions. Hands up, pal."

Biscuit whined slightly as he dropped the empty bowl to the table in front of him, and raised his forelegs above his head. Despite this, he kept his focus on the bowl, while Zappazmazoid's head swiveled to face the officers.

"We do not want any trouble," Zappazmazoid buzzed. "It seems there has been a misunderstanding."

"This is too weird, I should have gotten out of here earlier," a customer near the broad front window of the Maximum Burrito mumbled to his half-eaten meal.

No sooner had he finished speaking than the front window behind him exploded, and a tall, gaunt figure covered in fur, with a leering mouth of yellow teeth, burst through it, landing on the table and standing in the remnants of the man's meal with one taloned foot.

Everyone froze. The werewolf howled. The man seated

at the table dropped his mouth open, eyes wide, in utter shock, and with one clean swipe, the werewolf decapitated him.

"Massacre at the Maximum Burrito!!!" yelled the werewolf, in a horrifying, gravelly voice, then howled once more.

Behind the counter, Elvin and Darcy immediately began wiping down the prep area and boxing and storing ingredients. It was clear the restaurant was closing early today.

"Oh! Oh, shit!" stammered Bunson.

Mandel reached out to grab the lip of the counter, steadying themselves as their legs quivered beneath them.

Customers lost control– some screamed, some froze, some scattered– as the monster dropped off the table and advanced into the restaurant.

Bunson had collected himself, to a degree, and mustered a glimmer of his authoritative voice. "Freeze! Freeze right there, asshole!"

Dennison grimaced in dismissal, grabbing the arms of a patron that had remained rooted to their seat and wrenching them out of their sockets. Too late, the customer stood up, almost in reaction to the mutilation, and rotated in place, spraying the surrounding area and those still nearby with gouts of blood.

At the sight, the volume of screaming increased.

"Oh, no fucking way!" Bunson yelled, stepping in to close the distance between himself and Dennison, and unloading shot after shot into the werewolf.

Mandel stood from behind him and did the same, swinging to cover a wider angle, moving forward, and firing their weapon.

The horrible beast jerked with each shot and stumbled a few steps, but recovered almost immediately, the slugs popping out of his flesh the way the first few kernels in a popcorn air popper announce that the real action is about to begin.

"Shit shit shit," Bunson reeled off, stepping back.

"Fuuuuh ..." agreed Mandel as Dennison seized them by the front of their nice dress shirt.

"Mandel!" Bunson shouted.

Dennison lifted Mandel over his head, and then hurled them at an upward angle, crashing Mandel into the vent-work hanging from the ceiling deep behind the counter. Mandel hung tangled in the crush of pipes and tubing for a moment, and then it all crashed to the floor as Dennison turned his back to it, officer and ruined metal in an inter-mixed heap.

"Okay then," Bunson said, lifting his fists in a futile posture.

Dennison loomed over Bunson as the duo rotated in a sparring dance. As Dennison moved to block the entrance and Bunson backed further into the restaurant, the beast raised his arm and pointed over the counter, back to where Elvin and Darcy were trying to pick through the wreckage to uncover Mandel. Dennison spoke again.

"Stay right there Maximum Burrito people. I'm getting to you. I have a complaint about your service. And I'm hungry. I'm going to eat your asse-AH-ahwhooooooooo-OOOOOOOOO!!!!!!!"

Dennison's deep growl of a voice shifted up several octaves as his threat was interrupted. Bunson had a split second of confusion until he noticed that a foot had just demolished the werewolf's wolf testicles from behind, the toe of the foot having landed a perfect bullseye on the flapping scrotum, crushing it with devastating impact right up into the werewolf's hairy perineum.

"Ahoooowawoooawoooawoooo," Dennison cried, as if

mocking his own wolf howl with a high, sing-song voice as he stumbled side-to-side clutching his genitals and angling to get an eye on this new assailant.

Lazy Nations loaded up and dispensed another devastating kick to the werewolf's cupped hands so that his were-jewels were again battered flat.

"Damn," said Bunson.

Tears streaming from his blazing wolf eyes, Dennison sprang with incredible quickness toward Lazy Nations before she could wind up for a third kick to his swimsuit zone. He slashed his claws sideways, managing to land a blow that sent Lazy Nations spinning sideways into a solid trash receptacle, bringing both it and herself to the floor. Trash spread around her, comingled with the dropped and discarded food and personal items of the scattered diners of the Maximum Burrito.

Dennison loomed above her, fully focused on this new enemy, teeth bared and claws ready to strike.

He pounced.

EVANGELINE DOPPLER HAD a plan for the day. She had run a whole list of errands, and gotten them all done faster than she had thought she would. When she returned home, she had done so a full hour and a half earlier than she had anticipated she would. It gave her a thrill to squeeze in one extra errand, if she headed back out.

She grabbed the small oblong wooden box from inside her hutch, and hustled out to the jeweler.

"Heck, if I'm going out again, maybe I'll stop someplace and treat myself to dinner," thought Evangeline.

LAZY NATIONS SNATCHED the freshly polished silver spoon off the floor of the Maximum Burrito and plunged it deeply into Dennison's eye. It was one of a set, scattered from the small wooden box that had spilled from a customer's purse in her flight from Dennison's onslaught.

Dennison jerked backward, spasming, skin boiling and popping.

"Hey! Hey! Whoa!" yelled Bunson, scrambling out of the way of the dying werewolf as Dennison stumbled to the center of the restaurant, clear by an arm's length of anyone else.

Fur fell from Dennison's body, evaporating to dark ash before it hit the floor. He shrunk violently as his form fell back from lupine to man, bones cracking. His tongue shot around the outside of his quivering mouth, staying too large and long for the orifice as it transformed in regression more slowly but more violently than the surrounding flesh.

Dennison shit.

"OH GOD, MAN," Bunson yelped in disgust.

Finally, Dennison fell to the floor of the Maximum Burrito, lifeless.

Lazy Nations rose to her feet, and brushed her hands off against her knees before straightening fully and glancing up at the menu.

Darcy helped Mandel stand, extricated from the rubble where he had been thrown, while Elvin reached behind a shelf and retrieved a broom and dustpan.

"Hank," Mandel croaked, leaning for support against Darcy.

Bunson shook himself out of staring at the withered

form of the lanky, naked man at his feet, the handle of a silver spoon still jutting from one eye socket.

"Hank..." Mandel said again.

Bunson looked up. "Mandel...are you...?"

"I'll be fine. But...there," Mandel wheezed. They pointed to the deep corner booth of the restaurant. "Our other dog slipped out. Except...I have the feeling this guy was the one we were already looking for."

Bunson raised his eyes, exhaled, and nodded.

IN A MOUNTAINSIDE CLEARING, a second stone in a circle of five lit with a pale glow from within.

29

The air began to feel purple. It came on that night and continued on into the day and beyond.

30

Erskine and Romana humped slowly and rhythmically on the balcony outside the penthouse. Each of them used the other to get their rocks off, so it was going relatively well for them. Romana rode Erskine, and with each pulse, ripples of transformation cascaded across their bodies so that it was an equal and interleaved mingling of wolf and humankind.

Romana climaxed, paused, and swung herself off of Erskine, leaving him to finish by himself. She stood nude, surveying the skyline of the city.

The two had found it easy to persuade people to their whims since leaving the ritual on the mountain, like the bewitching glow of the full moon clung to them, ensorcelling the minds of those they encountered.

It was how they had found their way to the penthouse suite of the most luxurious hotel in the downtown area. They had ambled their way confidently into the lobby, spoke to a fawning attendant behind the desk, then an unctuous manager, and then took up residence in the penthouse without a reservation or a clear agreement for how they would pay for their stay of an unbounded length.

That had been the gift Mr. Moon had seemingly given to the pair, with the unseen light of the full moon flaming behind them at every encounter. If they wanted something and spoke it, it would be given, as long as they merely said it and didn't offer a threat or a fight. Romana and Erskine could glide the surface of the water of humankind, as long as they didn't stop to break it themselves.

Romana looked back over her shoulder as the front door of the suite buzzed.

Curious, she reentered the suite, drew the drape across the glass of the balcony window to obscure Erskine continuing to work on himself, and slipped on a robe to approach the door.

Opening it, she came face-to-face with a middle-aged bellhop pushing a room service cart.

"Steak tartare and champagne," offered the bellhop. "The kitchen got the idea you and mister Laloupe would be wanting something, so here you go."

"Mmm. Yes," Romana replied.

She stepped aside, and the bellhop pushed the cart into the foyer of the room, glanced at Romana briefly, then turned again to the door and left, closing it behind him. Romana did not tip.

Something had shifted that evening, both Romana and Erskine felt it. It was what had likely inspired their tryst, a strange nudge from the outer world that the nature of things had transformed, increasing the energy that sparked in the flesh and bones of werewolves. The full moon had become fuller.

This is interesting, Romana thought, as the faint sound of rhythmic slapping drifted in from the balcony. She picked up one of the champagne flutes. *We didn't even have to ask. We didn't even have to think about asking.*

31

Toby Chompers had been living in the sewer for years, since he had been flushed down the toilet by his owner when the gator had started to get a little bit too big.

Since then, Toby Chompers had been carving out a modest but happy existence, gliding through the subterranean pathways, eating trash and the occasional escaped chicken from the nearby processing plant.

It had become a routine, and the route he tended to take as he moved about was essentially a circuit, the same sights, sounds, and smells echoing about as he swam.

This was new, though, purple and green foliage crawling down and across the stonework from above. The vines and flowers rippled and swayed in an invisible underground breeze, and Toby was drawn by the heat that bathed the vegetation.

Toby Chompers lugged his heavy frame out of the sewage, using his chest as a fulcrum while his little front legs wriggled and scrabbled. Hugging the wall of the tunnel, he burrowed forward and flipped onto his back, soaking in the warmth.

He squeezed his eyes tight and enjoyed the sensation on his broad belly, then popped one eye open as he heard a sound reverberate from down the sewer network.

Peanut, the old laboratory monkey that stalked around the sewers, had dropped into the tunnel and was approaching curiously but carefully, also attracted to what seemed to be a burgeoning tropical paradise beneath the city.

Toby Chompers closed his eyes again and stretched out his chin, the impression of a broad smile greeting the ever-nearer derelict monkey.

32

Shelly Weedler wandered around her street. She felt like she should try to talk to Dr. Desmond again, about what, she wasn't entirely certain, but it certainly felt like they needed to check in with one another.

Everything was horrible, to be sure, but at least when she was talking to Dr. Desmond or being questioned by those police officers, it felt like things were moving forward toward something. A resolution to whatever this all was, this weird, horrible night. Now, everything just felt sort of frozen in a moment of bizarre dysfunction.

The wall of black vans remained where they were, an impenetrable barricade around the parking lot leading to Dr. Desmond's mysterious garden.

Shelly made rounds to the assorted members of the emergency services, offering to answer any lingering questions they had, but none of them showed any interest, instead shuffling her off, claiming they weren't the people to whom she needed to speak.

~

ONE BY ONE, the non-black van vehicles and their crews departed the scene, leaving a sense of desolation on what would in other circumstances just be a normal, quiet night on the street. Nothing of note. The ambulance with Gloria had left, a squad car following it, and everything after that was more or less still.

Nobody had taken the blanket back, it was still hanging over Shelly's shoulders.

Rather than returning to her apartment– she didn't consider why, but it may have been that returning to the home she shared with Gloria, even as casual as the arrangement was, would make all of it come crashing in on her– she aimlessly perambulated down the sidewalk a bit.

Motion caught her eye from the alley to the right, a quick tangle of movement obscured by corners of buildings and dumpsters.

"Hello?" Shelly ventured.

The movement stopped.

"If you're worried about what was going on out here, it's pretty much all over," she continued as she inched into the alleyway.

Silence.

"You'd be right to want to hide, though. It was some pretty insane stuff. I don't really know the whole story, but I saw some of it, I can probably fill in some of the big picture, if it's freaking you out too much and you're just, like, hiding out back here."

Shelly had advanced a considerable distance off the street and into the alley. It was something she never would have done at this time of night if she was in her normal state of mind. If the world as a whole didn't just feel so strange.

She was just considering this when she noticed that

someone had approached behind her, cutting off her route back to the sidewalk.

In front of her, two additional slender figures emerged from hiding places on either side of the alley; they seemed naked, except that they had no orifices or markings of any kind on the outside of their bodies. She was sure that whatever was behind her was exactly the same.

Shelly didn't hesitate; she screamed at the top of her lungs.

The featureless trio sprang at her, hands raised, groping and clutching toward Shelly's neck.

Reflexively, Shelly raised her arms in what seemed like an attempt to either shield herself with, or even hide beneath, her blanket. The action also made her look up, through the little open hole of the funnel the blanket had made.

Through it, she saw a shape somersault above her, briefly blocking out the arcs of light haphazardly illuminating the alley.

Shelly pivoted the aperture in the blanket to follow the gymnast as they landed in front of her, kicking one of the other figures away and using the counterweight to slam an elbow back into the other figure.

"HOOMP!! HAAAAA–!" shouted Shelly's rescuer as they rained down their blows.

Shelly continued to use the clustered opening in the blanket as if she were looking through a spyglass at some distant scene, instead of something occurring within feet of her.

"HEET!! HOYT!!" cried the lone fighter, one exclamation for each spike they produced from a belt lined with the weapons. The fighter lunged forward, impaling the attackers, and as the spikes penetrated skin, a spout of chunky yellow-white soup erupted, accompanied by the sound of deflating balloons as they fell back, withering and flattening.

Shelly followed the motion through her framed viewport as the warrior ran back toward her and then, impossibly, *up* along the wall of one of the buildings, momentarily bending the will of gravity by 90 degrees in an ostentatious show of acrobatic ability.

Are they also wearing a blanket? Do we match? thought Shelly momentarily. Then it occurred to her what was happening here. *Oh. No. That's a cape.*

By then, the caped individual was dropping the remaining figure with two knees in its back, riding it to the ground, yelling, "GA-REEEEEEE!!" And then, with a final "HOOP!" the fighter drove a spike into the downed figure's back, inducing a volcano spray of gloopy emission and the same wet sound of discharge.

The victor stood, and turned with a pronounced motion toward Shelly.

Shelly dropped the blanket back to her shoulders and looked them up and down. Calf-high, stiff blue boots. Blue trunks. The belt, replete with silver, piton-like spikes. The cape was blue and hooded. Everything else was wrapped in tight bandages, including their face, although over their eyes was an opaque gemstone-shiny magenta kind of visor. Across their bandaged chest, they had a kind of brace shaped like one of those crosses from Hot Topic, the ones with that upside-down teardrop loop at the top.

"What the fuuuu—" Shelly began.

"I AM THE ANKH!" explained the Ankh, cutting her off. "I HAVE BEEN ENTRUSTED WITH THE TASK OF PROTECTING MANKIND FROM THE CLUTCHES OF THE MOON CREATURES. POOR MEN AND WOMEN

THAT HAVE FALLEN PREY TO THE LURE OF...THE
MOON!!! YOU ARE SAVED THIS NIGHT!"

"Oh wow. So shit like this is just going to keep happening," remarked Shelly.

The Ankh replied with a dramatic pose, and then park-
oured back and forth between the buildings of the alley,
upward and into the night.

33

G loria's body had been delivered to the city morgue, and had gone into a drawer (even though it didn't need all that space).

There was a little bit of hubbub when it came in, and an exchange of gallow's humor between the transmitters and receivers of her remains. The city morgue had seen quite a lot of ghastly and unusual customers over the years, but Gloria would still rate in the top five.

After that excitement, and the departure of everyone but the overnight lab tech, Rodrigo Lorenzen, the night had settled into its usual routine.

Rod was there to handle any receipts that happened to come up over the night, but otherwise had a never-ending, steady stream of data entry to handle at a pace he himself determined.

As such, Rod was kicking back behind the small wooden desk on which the morgue's desktop sat, both feet perched on a partially opened drawer. He paged through a magazine entitled SMASH!: Music for Everybody. It had a cover with four or five different photos jammed together, and a cornu-copia of type and typefaces thrown randomly across it.

"Bum, bu-gadda– bum," Rod was humming as the drawer scraped open.

Gloria's pelvis and legs had managed to push the drawer open, her upper body and arms flapping like a windsock in still air. Through some of the tears in the flesh, it was apparent that tiny flowers had bloomed on a mesh of violet roots.

Gloria's legs swung out from the drawer and dropped to the floor, stiffly hobbling to the door of the morgue. They bumped against it a few times trying to push it open– unfortunately, the door opened inward.

The legs backed up a bit and then charged forward, planting one foot against the door and bursting it open the wrong way on its hinges. Then they tumbled forward into the hall outside, hustling away with a bow-legged stride.

Rod watched all of this over the top of his copy of SMASH!: Music for Everybody magazine impassively and without movement other than flitting his eyes up to absorb the scene.

After the departure of Gloria's legs, he began slapping the breast of his lab coat, finally locating his pocket and withdrawing his phone. He held it out and held the button down until it dinged to acknowledge it was listening.

"Call Dr. Madison," Rod said evenly.

The phone rang as Rod put it to his ear, the answer coming on the other end after three and a half rings.

"Dr. Madison," Rod greeted his superior. "One of the bodies just got up and left."

There was no response from the other end of the phone.

"I thought I should probably call."

34

B unson and Mandel sat sequestered in a dark room at the station behind a simple wooden table.

Mandel winced and shifted uncomfortably– they weren't seriously hurt, but the small bruises and cuts and aches were adding up to be very unpleasant. Perhaps the worst, most discomforting thing to deal with was the giant grease splotch on the back of their shirt. Oily and making the shirt back slightly transparent, it kind of felt like it was just growing and growing, and every time Mandel leaned back against the seat, they felt a spasm of disgust and sat upright. The cascade of little pains ran like a train line of tiny shocks through their body.

Neither Bunson nor Mandel felt much of an inclination to talk– overall, they were both still in something of a state of shock. They had moved with ingrained precision to control the scene after the werewolf had been neutralized, but when back-up arrived, they had been relieved, and numbly received the news that they should return to the station for a very important debriefing.

Neither were sure precisely how much trouble they were

in; it's true that they had probably made some serious errors in judgment, but the nature of the circumstances they had endured across the evening would be difficult to see as anything but wildly exceptional. From the black vans and the biohazard and the imploded woman, to the talking dog with the robotic second head, to what appeared to be a real werewolf and its penchant for slaughter, it was beyond the reach of many lifetimes of expectations, all crammed into a few hours.

The door of the room swung open in front of them, and two individuals entered, dressed identically. Each wore a black leather jacket, black t-shirt, and dark jeans. Mirror shades hung at the neck of each t-shirt.

The woman spoke first. "Detective Bunson? Detective Mandel?"

Bunson gave Mandel a sidelong glance and nodded hesitantly. Mandel spoke for both of them. "Yeah, that's us. So, what kind of trouble are we in? Who are you?"

"Trouble?" the woman laughed. "You've seen some trouble, definitely, but you're not *in* trouble, not from us at least, unless things go really off the rails here. Which may seem like par for the course from what I hear of your night so far."

"This is Captain Boner, I'm Captain Hart," the man supplied. "And we're tracking the creature you encountered tonight. We're trying to assess what kind of threat it may present to the planet, so any information or impressions you can give us about it would be of some help."

"I don't think it's going to present too much of a threat now," Bunson answered.

"Yeah, that woman friggin' laid that thing out," Mandel agreed.

"What...? Oh, not the *werewolf*," said Boner.

"The robot head attached to the dog," said Hart. "We're

looking for more information about that individual. Those individuals."

"Not the werewolf? Not the–" Bunson stammered in disbelief. "You're not surprised at a werewolf? *A real werewolf??*"

The monumental outlandishness of the last few hours was beginning to crash across Bunson's brain.

"Not the werewolf," confirmed Hart.

"Werewolves, they're a known quantity. We know about them. We want to know about the robot head and the dog. His name is Biscuit, we understand. The dog," clarified Boner.

Bunson's mouth gaped as he looked back and forth between the pair of captains.

"Well," Mandel said, leaning forward. "We didn't have much time before the *werewolf* entered the picture. But the robot head and the dog, they were cooperative for those few seconds."

"Polite, even," agreed Bunson, somewhat vacantly, making an attempt to reenter reasonable conversational space.

35

"I don't see why I wouldn't believe you. It may sound like the details stretch credulity without the context. But it's you telling me this. You're you, and you're not given to flights of fancy or fabrications. You don't overstate, if anything you understate. And I trust you, so let's not waste our time contending with whether that's true or not. I believe you, and what is strange and left to be sorted out is all these other things you've encountered."

The woman adjusted in her ergonomic office chair, and swept her hair off her shoulder to behind her back. She listened to the voice through her earbuds and looked down at the laptop on the glass desk at which she was seated.

"The werewolf isn't a surprise, werewolves exist," she said.

She listened as the person on the other end of the line repeated that fact back to her.

"Yes, I realize, it is generally easier to consider them a fiction for most people, and so quote-unquote common knowledge puts us all in a position where the impression is that they are a fiction."

The woman tapped a few keys on her keyboard and leaned into her screen.

"This is interesting, I have access to CDC plus, and there is a huge spike in sightings and indicators for the area, even without the full moon. Somebody over there should be trying to reconcile this data. It doesn't make sense, raw, so there ought to be a rational, and possibly concerning, explanation for it."

She paused.

"Yes, well, given the way things work out for you, you should maybe consider carrying something silver around with you. I am not a huge subscriber to the ideas of coincidence and circumstance, but that would deny the trend that you have evidenced of having a knack for finding yourself, um, in the mix, on a regular basis. If there are more werewolves running around, not during the full moon– hm, that part does irk me, we have to figure that out– I think it is not without reason to expect that you're going to run into them.

"Mm-hm.

"Yes, I see, I can see where you would find it an expensive and inconvenient situation to be carrying around a silver weapon everywhere you go. That's fair. I still think you should consider it, figure out how you could do it as comfortably as possible. But I suppose you have managed to live in the kind of world where what you need falls into your hands whenever you need it. I find it dubious that past circumstance would indicate future circumstance for something like this...eventually you're going to flip a tails. But, that's your choice.

"No, no. The prospect of more werewolf fights is concerning, certainly. You would be within the bounds of reasonable behavior if thinking about it took up mental cycles. But I am more focused on the thing that attacked

Dad. The...what did he call it, the Quorbin? As good a name as any. Naming a new organism after a person has precedence. That's not something that I've ever heard of before this. There's *not* precedence for people turning into walking blocks of...cheese...and attacking their neighbors.

"I don't know, maybe there's stuff on forums or social or whatever that represents initial other encounters, that's what happens when something new rolls into the world. But then it's mostly nonsense for a while until there's some actual disciplined scholarship around it. We're just getting to have a handle on what's really going on with the Jersey Devil and the chupacabra and the moth men and the mole men.

"Yes, chupacabra.

"Anyway, I personally am not about to trust the internet for anything. It's a potential bell that something is happening, but then it's all pretty much noise. Reliable sources don't turn up anything; CDC plus doesn't have anything. Baxter's Index doesn't have an entry. Phantom Society doesn't have anybody that seems like they'd be an expert in 'cheese people.' I'll send a few inquiries out to the academics I know personally in extranormal fields of study.

"Basically, we're balanced between two things. We would like to raise a flag to somebody that had the expertise to handle this appropriately, but we don't need to alert anyone that would invade Dad's house and try to put you and him into isolation rooms or anything. It seems like whatever made Quorbin into a quorbin isn't structured like a communicable thing.

"Yeah, I think it's fine that you rolled it up and stuck it in the closet. We can hand it over to somebody if we figure out who that is.

"No, at this point, whatever is going to be in the, uh, rind, is going to be as useful as whatever stained the carpet. Especially if it's smelling so bad. I can only imagine Dad is being a headache about it. I don't know why he didn't call me. Well, I guess I do, he's not great at calling us about anything.

"Anyway, yeah. I've got it, I know a carpet cleaning place and they're not perverts. I'll give them a call, schedule it.

"Mm-hm, mm-hm. Well, I'll see what I can do, may not be much, but I'm glad you called, and I hope this gives you more of a sense of...stability about it? I think that's the right way to say it. Perspective? Well, thanks for calling. My hope is that it was a one off, very strange incident where Dad's neighbor turned into cheese and attacked him, and then you happened to run into a werewolf later that night. I really hate saying that. It's so dumb and weird.

"Yep. Bye-bye, love to you and Dad."

Crazy Nations double-tapped her ear bud and hung up the call with her sister.

She spun her chair in a circle, letting it slowly come to rest after it completed a full 360 degree rotation.

She hated things that didn't make sense, but making them make sense was an extremely satisfying exercise.

36

Shelly Weedler was fed up with feeling tossed around on a sea of freaky nonsense. She wanted to get a handle on what was going on and figure out if this was what reality was going to be like from now on, so she could have some kind of a plan for how she was going to live in it and be able to cope.

She had had a brief, terribly painful conversation with Gloria's father, who she had never met or spoken to before, arranging the logistics of when he and Gloria's brother could come to collect her things. They were lingering in devastating silence at the end of the call when he received an incoming call from the city's mortuary services, which he was obliged to take.

From then, Shelly had begun to search the internet for more information about the things she had witnessed over the previous evening. Flora-induced spontaneous implosion. A real life superhero calling themself The Ankh. Goo-filled, completely smooth creatures.

She had found a few posts and threads that sounded like they were talking about the latter, but it was clear they were all over the map with really nothing to offer her as she dove into them. Shelly had personal experience, and even if it was very little personal experience, if anybody nudged against the truth they didn't provide more of a close encounter than she had. Sightings at best, of three or four of them running down streets in the shadows. And most of it was wild speculation or outright lies, and an awful lot of vitriolic, semantic arguments based in nothing at all.

"The internet is useless," Shelly said out loud. "Alright, we're going to have to try something else out."

She typed: *Library with weirdest books* and accepted the autocomplete for *near me*.

"Yes, that's fine," she replied to her laptop, clicking the OK button in response to the *Allow to use my location* prompt from the search.

"Margaret...Thomas...Clareview...public library," Shelly read aloud, writing the words on the back of a receipt she had nearby, already hopeful, as if writing it down obliged the library to provide her some kind of assistance.

She finished reading the description. "A small public library, notable for its reference collection of the arcane and mystical, provided by grant in perpetuity by the Aristotle and Euma Oagi Fund."

Shelly closed her laptop.

"Sounds promising."

THE MARGARET THOMAS Clareview public library was pretty impressive from the outside. It was set back a bit from the buildings on either side to make space for the marble stairs that led up to the facade. Columns lined the front, forming an exterior roofed area, under which the book return sat. Dark wooden double doors marked the entrance..

I could believe this place has a collection of very weird books, Shelly thought as she ascended the marble stairs.

The inside, however, looked just like any other library.

Scanners at the door to deter intentional or inadvertent book thieves, a large desk to Shelly's right where the librarians criss-crossed each others' paths and assisted patrons. Rows of books. A wall of magazines, a line of computers. The librarian desk and entrance were on a perch, requiring a few steps down (or the ramp) to get to the body of the library. Shortly past the entrance, everything was carpeted in a color best described as drab...not gray but still colorless in its complexion. Tan? Although that wasn't exactly right either.

Shelly started down the stairs and then hesitated, looking back to the desk.

"Can I direct you to something?" asked one of the librarians.

"I was hoping to get access to the Oagi collection," Shelly ventured.

"*Oh, ahhh, gee,*" the librarian corrected, and then pointed over Shelly's right shoulder. "Head toward the left and back, that's the reference section, and then all the way in the back of that, the last two shelves in the corner."

"Do I...need permission or something?" Shelly asked.

"What? Oh, no." The librarian had already moved on to some kind of clerical work behind the desk, sorting and stamping both books and papers. "It's reference, so you can't check it out. But also, it's reference, so it's just in the reference section."

"Oh, okay," Shelly said, slightly disappointed to realize that she probably wasn't about to discover a sinister grimoire of intense cosmic power at a public library. She found the reference section, which had a table with a pair of giant unabridged dictionaries on Lazy Susan-like swivel mounts.

Shelly pressed on and located the two bookshelves forming the back corner of the reference section and the library. On the side of one was a little brass plaque that read "With Appreciation to the Aristotle and Euma Oagi Fund."

Shelly scanned across the books on the shelves. They were all unusually sized, either very large or very small, interleaved with one another. Some had short names like *Soap* or vaguely unsettling names like *Fat of the Land* or extravagant names like *Jej Du Ponzierre: A Study of the Folk that Live in the Small Corners.*

She was starting to feel a little silly, and almost entirely at a loss, when she, at random, withdrew a squat, thick volume from the shelf entitled *Prisoner of the Moon.*

"Hello, I think we are interested in the same book," buzzed Zappazmazoid from behind her.

37

A bulky shape climbed up the corrugated steel stairs of the oversized black van, sliding open the side door and stepping inside. Pushing the door closed, the broad figure unsnapped a few connections at its neck and lifted off the heavy mask of the safety suit.

Dr. Desmond exhaled, her head dwarfed by the suit cloaking her body.

She had, over hours and hours, been directing the Scalliard BioLab crew on how to extract and safely contain the contents of the garden. Hungry, crazed plants, fueled by animal blood and building up to release another deadly signal cloud of pollen in an effort to find their displaced queen.

"Martina," an expressionless voice greeted the doctor from a darkened sector of the van.

Dr. Desmond followed the sound, the slump of her body exaggerated by the suit engulfing it. "I've done what you asked," she reported wearily. "The specimens are contained, filed, and loaded up for transport to laboratory inspection."

"Excellent," replied Aemelia Grís, smoothing her pants

as she crossed her legs. "Martina, this is a mess, an ugly one."

"Wyatt's removal of the queen caused the–" Dr. Desmond stopped as Grís held up a single finger.

"It *revealed* the danger– and the potency– of the current state of the project," Grís said. "This is quite an acceleration, despite the ugliness, Martina. When you last indicated that an unknown factor had led to the possibility of a promising outcome, you understated it wildly. This should have had the attention of the company earlier. I say that in my capacity as a consultant."

Dr. Desmond glanced away from Grís, to the interior wall of the van.

"You had been working with this particular infusion for six months, yes?" Grís prodded.

Dr. Desmond shrugged the massive shoulders of the suit, objecting, "We only saw a rapid increase in result within the last couple of weeks. It seemed premature to call for additional attention when we couldn't even tell why it was happening. It felt inexplicable. Anomalous."

"You know which sort of animal blood you were working with, true?" Grís sniffed.

"I leave that to Dr. Schayles," Dr. Desmond explained weakly. "Her specialty is determining compatible and promising samples, and in the garden, we manage the infusion process, so we don't make the–"

"Martina, you know," Grís interrupted.

"It was an admixture of lupine, and..."

Grís raised her eyebrows, prompting the doctor to continue.

"...and...and...human," Dr. Desmond confessed, dropping her eyes to the floor of the van. "Questionable ethically if we were to be using the approach practically, but Dr.

Schayles's team supplied the blood, and to verify that the science could work at all, it was paramount to the project that we at least *explore* whether it could work or if it was simply a miscalculation at the theoretical stage…"

"Not an admixture," Grís corrected, casting aside all of Dr. Desmond's explanations. "It came from a single kind of creature. It, in fact, came from a single creature. You have been working with werewolf blood."

"Were…wol…" Dr. Desmond stammered, processing the idea, wheels turning in her mind.

"Yes, werewolf, and in case you haven't heard," Grís continued, "there has also been a pronounced amount of werewolf activity in the area in a time window that lines up with the increased 'success' you've measured. And that is without the influence of a full moon."

Dr. Desmond stared at Aemelia Grís, dumbfounded. Or horrified. Or both.

"Several parties are curious about these things, and how they may relate," Grís said. "And I consult with many of them."

38

The Ankh stood on the rooftop of a warehouse, their cape dramatically suspended by a cooperative jet of high flung air.

They stared at the Hotel Richmond several streets ahead of them, the den of their quarry. The Ankh could hunt quorbin (where had that name come from? The Ankh knew that was what they were called, but didn't know why, or why they knew it) every night. But more would come, lost souls like wheat to the thresher.

The beasts sequestered in the penthouse suite of the Hotel Richmond, however, were unique creatures. Even if more of their kind were made, those new monsters wouldn't have the power of the two transforming the hotel into their personal fortress.

Most people didn't even seem to notice, but from this vantage point, the Ankh could see it like traffic around an ant hill. The people that had been instructed to ignore the hotel slid around it, treating their curved path as if it were a straight line in their brains. And for those poor souls summoned to fortify the Hotel Richmond, they streamed right into it, offering their bodies and minds to the creatures inhabiting the building. Virtually quorbin themselves, for all the free will exhibited. And, ignored by passersby, *actual* quorbin gathered and stood in shifting clusters around the hotel walls.

The Ankh crooked their arm out in front of themself and squeezed their hand into a fist.

"FIENDS! THE ANKH WILL PREVAIL AND FREE YOUR SUBJUGATED THRALLS!!"

39

M arcy Egg was idly tracing her pencil across the boxes on a page of her jumbo crossword puzzle book in the office of the Royal Leisure Motor Inn. She had spent about half an hour on this one, managed to fill in about a quarter of it, and gotten to the point where she was feeling pretty stumped. It happened, it was part of her process. It's why she liked the jumbo book; she'd do as much as she could do, and then just turn the page and another puzzle was there. She wasn't going to be running out any time soon.

Marcy peered out the front window of the office, eyes unfocused to the distance, waggling the eraser end of the pencil in a sloppy circle.

"Chicken, chicken, chicken," she muttered absently, trying to take a last shot at figuring out one final clue.

Her hand froze and the pencil dropped, clattering onto the desk and then rolling off the edge to the floor.

The entirety of her body remained fixed in place, except her head, which traced the sight outside.

A pair of legs had walked up to the front of the Royal

Leisure Motor Inn, passed by the office, crossed the court-yard parking lot– and it was at this point that Marcy noticed the flapping, empty shape of an upper body trailing the legs like a broad tail. The legs walked over to number six. The door of number six opened, the legs disappeared inside, and the door closed again.

Marcy Egg blinked several times. She bent down to pick up the pencil, and returned to the page of her jumbo cross-word puzzle.

"Gonna have to do something about that, right, right, right," Marcy muttered under her breath.

"Chicken, chicken, chicken."

40

Romana strode back and forth on the wide landing of the gorgeous stairs of the Hotel Richmond.

The way the hotel was situated, the lobby allowed for all the initial traffic into the building. Along one wall was the long desk for checking in and transacting the hotel's business. Dotted across from that, on the other side of the wide open first floor, were various concierge desks and information kiosks, entryways to associated-but-not-affiliated bars and restaurants, and decorative installations. Running up the middle of the floor was tastefully appointed flora and water features, forming a kind of highway median between the bustle to either side, incoming traffic desk-side, outgoing and utility traffic separated by the divide on the other.

But the hotel proper really began on the floor above the lobby. Elevators were hidden away behind the staircase on the lobby floor, and presented themselves as gilded portals to the luxury of the hotel only on the next floor, which also opened itself widely, but in a much more tranquil fashion.

Conference rooms abutted the open area of the elegant onset of the hotel, keeping their activity sequestered away.

The massive stairway between the lobby and second floor was covered with a lush crimson carpet, each stair edged in gold. Halfway between the two floors, the staircase was split by a sizable landing, a half ellipse where the curved stairs paused, then opted toward a straight-lined arrangement to the next floor.

It was on this landing that Romana addressed her servants and followers, the gathered denizens of the Richmond Hotel, using it as a stage, or perhaps a pulpit. Erskine stood behind her off to one side. The two werewolves, though in human form, barely disguised their bodies, each with just a sliver of golden fabric draped across themselves.

"You. Are. Mine." Romana thundered across the lobby below.

The gathered humans let out a cheer. The quorbin that mingled amongst them seemed to grovel in a vaguely obscene way at the words.

"This place, whatever it was called before, is no longer that place. It is the Castle of the Moon. And we," Romana continued, "are your masters.

"You have felt it, you have been drawn to us, we have called you to us. He–" Romana pointed to Erskine and then to herself, "and I are the blessed, the special. We are among those who summoned Mr. Moon to this world, and we have been rewarded for that act. You are a part of that reward.

"We make a place here that Mr. Moon could rule from, if he so chose. But there will be some who defy us. We feel it. And from those, you must prepare to defend our home."

Again, the humans cheered and the quorbin quivered with insipid delight. Erskine raised his arms behind Romana.

"They will come! And they will perish!!!" Romana bellowed, punching the air, her hand gnarled into a claw.

41

S helly Weedler was handling this way more calmly than she would have ever guessed she might have.

She sat on a circular rolling stool with her back to the shelves that represented the collection provided by the Aristotle and Euma Oagi Fund. In front of her, Biscuit sat like a dog, tongue happily panting out of his mouth, as Zappazmazoid's head, level to her own, met her eyes.

"What is...well, what the fuck is going on?" Shelly asked, allowing her exasperation to flood out. "I mean, it seems like you'd know? You know? Why did my roommate blow up. Or, blow in, or whatever, because of...plants? What are these gross things without faces running around? Why is there a... fucking...fucking, *mummy superhero* running around? And you. You're...a...robo-dog? Conjoined robo and dog? Why did everything get so *weird* all of a sudden?"

"I can see why you may find all of this overwhelming, given how you have experienced reality up to this point. And you did not even mention the surge in werewolf activity," hummed Zappazmazoid sympathetically.

Shelly stared at Zappazmazoid. "Werewo...what? The fuck?"

"Are you familiar with the duality of matter?" Zappazmazoid queried, harmonics bathing the question in a tinkle of sound.

"...Matter?" Shelly repeated weakly.

"Matter," confirmed Zappazmazoid. "The duality of matter. At a certain scale, matter behaves as a particle. Solid, substantial. What you might call realistic. However, observe matter at another scale, a more minute scale and it begins to flout expectations, it begins to behave as a wave. A flowing action that you may deem fantastic. Matter is both of those things, and you have become accustomed, at the scale of your perception, to expect it to be just one of these things. Empirically, that is reasonable. In actuality, it is incorrect."

"Okaaaaaaaaaay," Shelly said.

"An entity that has the capacity to reprioritize the behavior of matter...of reality as you would perceive it...to be more of the wave than of the particle at the scale of biological consciousness recently escaped from its prison within the concept captured by the physical embodiment of the Moon."

Shelly put her face in her hands.

"There are creatures, werewolves per the designation of human cultural attribution, that are representative of the influence of this entity. The book in which we both have expressed interest is the essential detail of this, but a cadre of these creatures recently enacted a procedure, a ritual, that created a gateway, and released this entity from its prison. The werewolves made themselves a gate which released the entity, and the entity is changing the nature of matter, toward the behavior of the wave. To be very simplistic, in answer to your question, everything has gotten so weird all of a sudden because this entity has arrived on your planet, and the binding to its prison, the construction limiting its influence, is eroding. Reality is only going to get weirder the longer it has the opportunity to flourish. I had been charged to stand sentry at its prison, and now that it has been released, it is my duty to return it to that prison as a measure against a catastrophic shift in the behavior of reality at the scale of your perception."

Biscuit let his mouth hang open, tongue out, in a way that made it look like he was smiling, having a great time with all of this.

"Aaaaaargh," Shelly breathed, her head spinning a little at the explanation, which maybe had explained some things, but also made her feel like it plunged her into even darker, deeper, stranger waters. She was having trouble figuring out in which direction the surface lay, and felt like she needed to swim toward it, but the effort could just as easily plunge her deeper and deeper into the suffocating darkness.

"Okay. Okay. So, these...fucking *were*wolves...open a gate that let this 'entity' out, and now that it's out, it's making all this stuff happen. And stuff is going to keep happening and keep happening more as long as it's out there. So, what? We need to kill all these werewolves so that there's no more gate?"

Shelly was a little surprised at herself, that she had gotten so flippant about the idea of death and murder, even if she was talking about the murder of a werewolf. Werewolves, plural, it sounded like.

"BzzzzHmmmmm," Zappazmazoid sounded as if they were trying to respond diplomatically. "No. No, actually. It is doubtful that the full collection of werewolves had complete cognition of what they were doing when they executed the procedure. It is likely that only a minority of the group understood the implications of what they had initiated. The entity has already utilized the gate to escape the prison. Destruction of the gate is now what it desires to guarantee its ongoing freedom. While the gate still exists, the entity can be put back into confinement. If the gate is destroyed, there is no way to return it to where it has been held. It needs to be captured prior to the demise of its servants, which it is no doubt conspiring to hasten."

"Fu-huuuck," Shelly said. "All right. Wow. Okay. So, you seem to know all this stuff already, why do you need the book? What about the faceless, like, pudding people? What about the superhero...the Aaaahhh...I forget. Something like 'the Ant?'"

Zappazmazoid tapped the book, *The Prisoner of the Moon*, with Biscuit's paw. "Take a look."

Shelly flipped the heavy volume open and let the pages spray randomly to a stop. She let her eyes fall on the text.

The quorbin are those that have fallen into the thrall of Moon, rejecting allegiance to the reality which made their physical forms.

"So, that's talking about the pudding people?" Shelly surmised. The word "quorbin" in the text felt like it was freshly typed compared to the faded print on the rest of the aged pages.

"That explanation is adequate. BzHm...quorbin," ruminated Zappazmazoid. "As the dynamics of reality shift, those individuals compelled to feel detachment from the behavior of existence as-is, have the opportunity to discard it, even if it is to the detriment of themselves, even if it is to the detriment of humankind as a whole. They permit themselves to become monsters, to them it is more satisfying to be correct the way they want to be correct than to be human anymore, and, perhaps, occasionally be wrong."

"Ugh, they're 'Do my own research' people," Shelly said.

Zappazmazoid's unmoving features did a good job of looking at her blankly.

"As for your superhero, it is likely to be another side effect of the transformation of reality. Immediately after the release of the entity, one of the five pillars of the gate fell, and the lunar energy began to infuse the planet. Only enough to agitate and empower the immediate members of the werewolf collective, and perhaps *some* stray other anomalous activity. I personally witnessed the fall of the second pillar of the gate, which would have been enough to begin to cause serious ripples in the fabric of actuality. I was not prepared for that and was not able to prevent it. But with only slightly more than half of the gate intact, it is very likely that occurrences that you would view as highly unusual, such as your superhero, would be asserting themselves. You ought to expect more than that, and if more of the gate falls before the entity can be captured, the experience of substantive reality will be even more diluted."

"Fannnnnntastic," Shelly murmured sarcastically.

"As for the book," Zappazmazoid concluded, "I hope that I have shared with you enough information, and at a level of clarity that would be more immediate than if you should read the text, and therefore that you feel comfortable releasing it to me. It is true that I already possess the data the book would share, but the book is also a device which may permit me to capture the entity and transmit it back to its prison, as long as the gate remains open. As you can likely assess, my physical form has been compromised, and the utilities I would normally have at my disposal to execute a capture have been eliminated. The book, as a tool, restores some semblance of my capacity to serve as a jailor and warden for the escapee."

Lazy Nations strolled into the foyer of the Margaret Thomas Clairview library. Her eyes drifted across the bulletin board on the wall to the right. It was festooned with a wide range of material, from advertisements to help-wanteds to lessons. Her eye caught for a moment on a small, out-of-place *Have You Seen Me* flier for a lost hiker by the name of Joe Hickock, before she continued on into the library and waved to get the attention of the librarian behind the desk.

"Hi. My sister sent me here to look at a book she said you've got. It's called *Prisoner of the Moon*?" Lazy Nations inquired.

The librarian acknowledged her with a nod, putting a book atop a small stack of its brethren and then typing several words into the computer.

"It's not here," Shelly Weedler said from down the steps into the library.

The librarian paused, looked between Lazy and Shelly, then turned away from the computer, retrieved the book she had just deposited, and retreated back into an anonymous bubble of clerical work.

"Not here?" Lazy Nations asked Shelly.

"Sorry," Shelly confirmed. "It was here. But it's not here now. A dog checked it out. I'm Shelly Weedler, by the way. I bet you've been seeing a lot of pretty weird stuff too, if you're looking for that book specifically. Pudding people–quorbins? Or plants that explode people? Or a superhero–maybe werewolves?"

"Someone checked it out? Wasn't it in the reference section?"

"Yeah, it is. Was."

"My sister says you can't check out reference books, you have to look at them in the library."

"Maybe that's the rule for people? But I guess it's different for dogs."

"What?" Lazy Nations asked.

"I guess they have different rules for dogs. Maybe dogs can check out reference books. So that Biscuit could check it out," Shelly theorized.

The librarian, giving no indication of hearing the exchange, opted not to weigh in on the matter.

42

The familiar yellow and green of the Real Buddies Mobile logo shone down from the roof of the store onto the sidewalk outside, adding a little bit of color into the streetlit night. Inside, a couple revisited the conversation that had brought them into the store, seeing as how the clerk helping them had gone to grab a couple of phones and a tablet for doing all the paperwork.

"I think this is a really good idea. I just don't want to go through what we went through because of our *phones*. That's silly! And, what, we were fighting for days over it, and it was just our phones," one of the pair said to the other. "And I saw on the internet that one of the reasons that can happen is people being on two different networks. And the internet also says that this place is one of the best places to go, if you're switching from another provider. And we both are."

The other partner shrugged, not one to try to debate the internet, as behind the two, a pack of nude, smooth, feature-less interlopers sped out of the night toward the front windows of the store.

The first quorbin bounced off the glass of the window

and rebounded back down onto the sidewalk, spinning on its knees from the force. The resounding *thunk* of the impact was enough to draw the attention of the employees and customers milling about the Real Buddies Mobile store, however, and they were already screaming by the time the second quorbin shattered the glass of the window and stormed inside, rivulets of milky fluid streaming from the numerous cuts and gashes across its otherwise unblemished frame.

More quorbins followed, bursting through glass or following the paths cleared by others in the pack. A dozen rampaged into the store, a sick mirror to the number of humans gathered there.

One quorbin stumbled into a man in a plaid button-up who had, moments earlier, been perusing tablets at the front of the store– the quorbin hooked the man's lower jaw, and ripped it off like tearing a tag from a pillow. The man fell to his knees, tongue lolling, and then toppled all the way over.

A smaller-statured individual got picked up by the neck and ankles, and whirled broadside, the attacking quorbin using the person as a battering ram to demolish spinner racks of phone cases.

An employee stood in the center aisle of the store in a yellow polo shirt, hands on each side of their head, and let out a scream of abject terror. "AAAAAaaaaaAAAAAAaaa-AAAAAAAAAaaaa–"

It was interrupted by the sound of shattering glass, the penultimate remaining window of the storefront splintering to pieces as The Ankh swung through it in a breathtaking aerial display.

The costumed hero landed on a table of demo paraphernalia in a crouch. Then, one knee bent, The Ankh traced a large circle with their outstretched foot as they swiveled to survey the full vantage of the store. Everything slowed for that moment.

Then the room sprang back into brutal action.

The Ankh kicked a combination color copier-fax machine (the last model available from its manufacturer, and the last model offered by the store– in fact, the last single unit available in the city) from the table, and it connected with the head of a quorbin throttling an employee, the featureless bulb immediately bursting like a pale yellow grape full of milk.

"GHEEEEE-YAAAAAAH!!!" cried the Ankh, leaping from the table and scissor-kicking quorbin left and right.

"GOO! GRURN!! GA-SHAAAAAAAAB!" the Ankh bellowed, felling a monster on each shout.

The quorbin, at first a pell-mell of random violence against the denizens of the Real Buddies Mobile store, began to scramble as one in an attempt to flee the store and their lethal hunter.

The Ankh brought down the two quorbin that tried to rush past either side of them, caving the torso of one with their foot while using both hands to propel the head of the other into the lip of a nearby table, its grotesque creamy filling erupting in a plume from the top of its skull.

Balanced on one leg, the Ankh pivoted to face the fiendish menaces as they raced away into the night. Retrieving two silver spikes from their belt, the Ankh pitched them both unerringly, cape flaring behind them, and dropped another pair of quorbin on the sidewalk outside the store.

"ARR-FYAAAAAAH!!" The Ankh howled as the spikes found their marks.

The Ankh took one final scan of the store and then

sprang forward, slamming through the last remaining store window in a glittering cascade of glass splinters, spinning around one of the emptied window frame supports and parkouring against it upward to the store's sign, pulling themselves up and out as if onto a giant neon pommel horse, and then disappearing once more into the night.

"HOOP-DJEE-YAAAA!!!" The sound floated down from the top of the store as the Ankh vanished.

The people left standing in the store whimpered and wept in the aftermath, as those uninjured and not plunged into an abyss of abject shock glanced around, bewildered.

The jawless man lay on his back at the front of the store, his eyes wide open and bugged out – without the lower half of his face, he gave an impression that he was sporting a giant, open-mouthed smile, like he was overwhelmed with appreciation at the demonstration of superheroism that had just transpired.

SHELLY WEEDLER, understandably, had not gotten much sleep since watching the top half of her roommate implode. But she was exhausted, and having had achieved some modicum of explanation for why things were happening like they were, however bizarre, she finally submitted to the satisfying tug downward toward true, deep sleep as she lay back in her bed.

"SHELLY WEEDLER!" a voice boomed into her room, blaring in volume but with the audacity to assume the cadence of a confidential conversation.

"Oh no, please," Shelly moaned, slapping an arm over her eyes. After a brief, hopeful pause in which she prayed that she would be left alone, Shelly peeked out from under her arm to get a look at the window across her room facing her bed. Outside stood a silhouette cutting a posture of bravado and stoic power. Arms bent at the elbow, hands on hips, legs apart in a vee, shoulders back, chin up– and, of course, the outline of a cape flaring into the night.

"SHELLY WEEDLER!" The Ankh repeated. "IT IS I, THE ANKH! NEFARIOUS BUSINESS IS AFOOT! THE CREATURES FROM WHICH I SAVED YOU PROLIF-ERATE ACROSS OUR FAIR CITY! AND I HAVE DISCOV-ERED THEIR MASTERS! MS. WEEDLER, THESE CREATURES ARE SIMPLY PAWNS OF BEASTS THAT ARE BOTH HUMAN AND WOLF! AND I KNOW OF THEIR LAIR! THEY HAVE ENSORCELED THE SLEEPING EYES OF THE COMMON PERSON AND SIT AMONGST US ALL UNDISTURBED...AT THE HOTEL RICHMOND!! YOU MAY NOT EVEN REMEMBER THAT THIS HOTEL HAS EVER EXISTED SUCH IS THE POWER OF THEIR UNNATURAL DECEPTION!"

Shelly hadn't ever really heard of the Hotel Richmond, but she didn't think it was a big deal that she didn't know the name of every hotel in the city.

"I MUST DISPENSE WITH THESE FIENDS FOR THE SAKE OF THE CITY! I WILL SUCCEED! BUT I MAY NOT SURVIVE! I FEEL CLOSER TO YOU MS. WEEDLER THAN ANY OTHER! I FEEL WE HAVE A CONNECTION! I HOPE THAT WE WILL SEE ONE ANOTHER AGAIN AFTER I COMPLETE MY MISSION! BUT KNOW THAT IF WE DO NOT, YOU HAVE TOUCHED THE HEART OF THE ANKH!"

"Is this, like, something we could discuss a little later?" Shelly asked sleepily.

"I AM OFF! I WILL SLAY THE TWO WEREWOLVES

ROOSTING WITH THEIR MINIONS AT THE HOTEL RICHMOND!!!!! GUR-WHHEEEEEEEEEEE!!"

"Slay the..." Shelly repeated before her eyes popped open wide. She leapt from her bed, suddenly awake, and rushed to her window.

"No! No! No!" she cried after The Ankh, already gone. "NO! Don't do that! For...for fuck's sake."

Shelly stood, completely at a loss in her v-neck t-shirt and pajama pants. She wished she had Zappazmazoid's phone number, or the number to call his head directly, or whatever it would take to get in touch with him.

She strode back over to her bed and picked up her phone from the nightstand, opening her contacts, typing a couple letters, and then tapping one of the autocompletes.

"Hi," Shelly greeted the voice on the other end. "This is Shelly Weedler, from earlier. I thought we kind of left off, like, on the same page, and some, well, some shit just came to the forefront that I felt like I needed to tell *somebody*. Sorry, I guess you're my somebody."

Shelly listened to the response, and then nodded in agreement to it.

"Well, that superhero I told you about just came over to my house."

An interjection from Lazy Nations tumbled out on the other side of the call.

"YEAH, I know! *My house*! I think they're in love with me or something. Stupid shit. Well, that's annoying, but get a load of this, they told me they know where TWO werewolves are and that they're going to go kill both of them."

Another remark from Lazy Nations.

"Yeah, we're all fucked then. I can't imagine what it would be like if we got *one* dead werewolf weirder than we're already at, much less two. Two dead werewolves weirder?

Like, what, are we all going to turn into, like, puppets or something? Geez-a Louise. Fuck.

"Yeah, yeah, they told me. The Hotel Richmond. Apparently the werewolves made, like, a clubhouse or something there to be all creepy with the quorbin things. So the...honk...the oink? The, ah, the onk is going to go fuck them up. Murder them. There.

"No, I don't know where it is, I've never heard of it. Where? Let me look at my computer."

Shelly pulled her laptop over onto her bed, cracked it open with one hand, and clicked on a browser tab. "Give me those cross streets again.

"No, there's nothing there, that doesn't work. What? Yeah...wow, yeah, that's weird. Shit, I see. The math on the street doesn't work for nothing to be there...and the blocks to the east and west don't work on the grid if that's how those cross streets...whoa. I see it. I see it now. The Hotel Richmond. Fuck. That is wild. You didn't have any problem remembering that?

"You're what? Oh, wow, I just wanted to talk to somebody. I didn't mean to obligate you to...wow, alright. Okay."

Shelly put the tips of her fingers against her lower lip, then nodded her head again.

"Okay. I'll meet you there, then, I guess."

43

C aptains Boner and Hart were heading out of the station, escorted by Bunson and Mandel. The quartet had gone over everything the officers had seen, and were in alignment over the desire to get circumstances under control. There was information that the representatives of the Secret Rapid Defense Force couldn't divulge to Bunson and Mandel, but for the field of play that was visible to all parties, they saw eye-to-eye. The four had worked together to figure out the motivation for the werewolf attack, and try to piece together every detail of the interaction with the dog-borne robot head. It had ended up being a long conversation.

Just as the group neared the end of the restricted area of the station, they were stopped in their tracks by a voice emanating from a doorway. "Richard, Veronica...we need to talk."

All four stopped, turning toward the open door.

"Grís," Captain Boner hissed from between her clenched teeth.

As if compelled to appear, Aemelia Grís stepped into the

frame. She spoke as much to the empty air of the hallway, as to Bunson and Mandel. "We won't be requiring you officers, you're dismissed."

Captain Hart warned them off with his eyes, a considerable amount of implication in his glance. In unison, Bunson and Mandel shrugged, backing off from the exchange and taking their leave.

"We have the room," Grís said, gesturing for the captains to join her.

Hart walked past Boner to the open doorway, their eyes meeting only briefly. Boner fell into pace behind him, pulling herself together to hear whatever Grís had to share. At best, Boner expected it to be condescending and insulting. At worst...it could be very, very bad news indeed.

"JUST TO LEVEL SET HERE," Grís began, "I am fully aware of what you are doing here, and what you are pursuing."

She scanned the painstakingly neutral faces of the captains and proved it by continuing, "You are in pursuit of an extra-planetary visitor, or what remains of them after an airborne encounter with Richard here. A piece of that visitor– the head– managed to reach the surface of the planet, seems to have achieved mobility via a chocolate labrador retriever, and so represents extra-planetary interests and a probable threat. Your mission is to neutralize that threat."

The captains dropped their shoulders as a kind of confession, relaxing into a more open posture, Grís having spelled out exactly what they were doing.

"I am in possession of information that I have the leeway to share. It may provide you with extra dimension to your endeavors," Grís asserted, "that may, in fact, give you the direction you need to complete your mission.

"In my capacity as a consultant for various interests, I have had the opportunity to accrue insight from disparate sources that all add up to an interesting, albeit troubling, picture."

Captain Hart put his hand to his chin, listening. Captain Boner crossed her arms.

"You undoubtedly have some awareness of the unusual magnitude of werewolf activity the area has been seeing. Outside, even, of the encounter those officers just witnessed. There has been an unprecedented surge, considering the absence of a full moon to induce it.

"In conjunction with the timing of that surge, a botanical research laboratory utilizing werewolf blood experienced unexpected success after a lengthy run with no useful results. Well, technically," she reconsidered, "success may be a mischaracterization, given their goals. Timed to the werewolf activity, the results from the study quickly went from overwhelming to deadly. They accidentally grew a semi-sentient, deadly weapon that seeks itself out. And they were trying to set a baseline for weather-resistant food."

The captains took it all in, tightly nodding to show that they were following along, and occasionally glancing at each other.

"And that's where your visitor comes in...all of this happens, and then, almost immediately, your visitor shows up. According to my sources, the belief is that your extra-planetary individual is marshaling a werewolf uprising and augmenting it with hybrids in the vegetable kingdom."

Captain Hart let out a long slow breath. Captain Boner put her hand on her head.

"The imminent danger here is obvious," Grís pressed on.

"But we have an opportunity to meet it head on...your adversary seems to have gathered additional werewolf and other supplementary ally forces in a building in the center of the city. Formerly the Hotel Richmond. Now psychically screened from perception both directly and indirectly, the extra-planetary entity and its forces are fortifying their stronghold there. Here, you'll see what I mean. Look right here at this map, right here, and see if you can see the Hotel Richmond."

Captain Hart and Captain Boner stared at the tablet Grís had placed in front of them. Both narrowed their eyes, furrowed their brows, and peered hard at the map on its face. Each of them looked at it, back up to Grís's eyes, and back down to the tablet slightly out of rhythm with one another. Hart gave up first, shrugging his shoulders, and sitting back in his chair. Boner took several more seconds, then slowly eased back away from the tablet, lifting her eyes to Grís.

"Right, I think you'll see what I mean. Look here," she said, raising her forefinger to be level with her eyes. "And follow." Grís slowly moved her finger down and onto the tablet, pointing. Hart and Boner focused on its tip and tracked it onto the lit surface.

"I'll be damned," Boner muttered with muted amazement. "There it is. The Hotel Richmond. That's some trick."

Hart grunted in agreement, then looked back to Grís, "That's the target then."

"I believe that to be the case," agreed Grís. "And now, with some discretion, you may read in your law enforcement friends. We should all want to eliminate what has been gathered at the Hotel Richmond."

Grís stood, slapped the cover closed over the tablet, and headed around the seated captains to the door. She lingered in front of it for a beat, and reflected, "At least they've done us something of a favor here. Nobody notices the Hotel Richmond anymore, so nobody is going to notice an all-out military scale assault on the Hotel Richmond."

Grís paused again, then added, "*If* you and your superiors deem that to be the appropriate scale of response. As a consultant, all I can do is provide a recommendation here."

Grís stepped out of the door. "But that is my recommendation."

44

Romana stood on the balcony of the penthouse
suite, looking over the marble rail to the street
below.

"So, they mean to test us," she spat, running her eyes
over the semi-circle of heavily armored vehicles assembling
in front of the Castle of the Moon, né the Hotel Richmond.
"Let them shatter themselves against the rocks of our
shore."

"They found us," Erskine commented, with a hint of
warning. It would not do to underestimate the forthcoming
assault. If the forces below were able to locate the Castle of
the Moon, they were possessed of unexpected and unfore-
seen abilities.

Romana scoffed, turning to snarl at Erskine. The reach
of their minds had grown like a carpet of moss over the
consciousnesses in the Castle of the Moon, and she felt
certain that any human entering the building would
succumb to the spread.

Let them come and add to our strength, she thought.

Erskine raised his eyebrows skeptically as Romana brushed past him.

"I won't deny you the opportunity for the hunt," she added aloud, falling into a lope as she began to transform. "We will ravage what we wish, and take whatever is left for our own."

Erskine smiled, and the smile widened and bled as his bones began to crack and stretch.

Bunson cleared the corner of a heavy-set vehicle to meet with Mandel and the officer in charge of the tactical team. He nodded at his partner and gave a quick, casual acknowledgement to the helmeted and armored individual next to Mandel, tapping his forefinger against his brow.

"Thanks for bearing with my old-fashioned caution," Bunson offered as he joined them. "I just felt better taking a quick jog around and seeing the set-up with my own eyes."

The third of the trio, Tactical Lead Axiola Verboga, nodded wordlessly, and looked at the towering Hotel Richmond before them.

For their part, the law enforcement team was tasked with keeping the opposition pinned inside the hotel, but were under strict orders not to enter themselves. They had coordinated with the representatives of the Secret Rapid Defense Force, and the ground rules had been strict and explicit: whatever was in the hotel needed to be kept there at all costs, but law enforcement should not cross the threshold of the hotel. The SRDF would stack an attack on top of the law enforcement barricade, and then, when they were convinced that the suppression had been successful, they would send in a retrieval team for the particular and exceptional targets bivouacking in the hotel.

That retrieval team was sequestered in the largest of the vehicles, a domed, treaded giant sitting behind the front line of the tactical vehicles which blinked occasional red and blue lights on its exterior.

"All right then, we're good to go," Mandel said, speaking into the com. "We're kicking off the first wave, synced up with the timeline."

Dropping the com, Mandel turned to Verboga and reiterated, "Confirmed, we're a go."

Verboga gave a sharp nod and pressed a circular button that had laid flush with the exterior surface of their helmet; there was a small electronic buzz as Bunson and Mandel heard Verboga issue the command. "Light it up."

From the arc of tactical vehicles, a staccato cascade of heavy thumps compelled Bunson and Mandel to involuntarily crouch for cover as a rain of knockout gas projectiles peppered the front of the hotel, breaking windows and, in places, punching through walls and doors.

Seconds later the hiss and fog of the chemical cloud began to roll out of the hotel, lit by the spotlights directed on it from the vehicles.

Bunson patted Mandel on the shoulder and pointed toward the hotel at about the level of its second floor.

"What is that?" Bunson asked, tracking what appeared to be a caped figure sliding along a highwire to the hotel.

"Wha...?" Mandel said as the figure dropped off the line, disappearing into the billowing blanket of gas and out of view.

∽

INSIDE THE CASTLE of the Moon, the thralls of Romana and Erskine gathered on the great lobby floor, preparing to engage whatever attackers breached the main access point and fall back, drawing their foes up toward the staircase landing, where the werewolves would meet them.

As the projectiles broke through into the lobby and rained down, the collected human and quorbin army prepared to execute the plan, thinking the volley to be a prelude to a physical onslaught by invading forces. Initially bracing themselves, an awkward atmosphere began to pervade their clustered groups as they waited, the acrid fog steaming into the vast room from multiple landed devices.

"GAS!!" yelped a concierge, unhelpfully, before passing out, his face slapping roughly against the marble floor.

The humans began to scramble and drop, rendered unconscious by the knockout gas as they shouted and leaped around aimlessly.

But the quorbin, transformed as they were, and no longer needing to breathe– a detail unknown by the opposition– remained ready to battle.

"Outside, end them!" an enraged Romana commanded from the lush landing atop the first circular flight of stairs.

The quorbin surged forward, breaking through windows and doors to engage the forces outside the Castle of the Moon. As the massed body of them charged out, stepping without notice over and on their unconscious human companions, the thin whistling sound of someone quickly traversing a zipline floated from overhead.

The Ankh dropped from above into the tail grouping of quorbin, and began kicking, punching, and spiking the monsters, moving through them toward their werewolf targets.

"HAR-GLAA!! KEE-OOOSH!!" the Ankh yelled.

Romana, a few steps down, climbed back up onto the landing to observe the newcomer.

"AGGA-DEE-OOOOHG!" the Ankh shouted, as they swung their arms outward in unison, spiking the head of a quorbin to each side. As the creatures parted around the Ankh to forge forward to the battle outside the walls, some formed an eddying current, looping back and encircling the whirling superhero in an enclosure of bodies.

The Ankh fought on, felling quorbin while pushing the orbit of enemies around them forward toward the awaiting werewolves.

OUTSIDE, the wave of quorbins sprang out of the Hotel Richmond and charged toward the arc of vehicles.

"Whoa, whoa," exclaimed Mandel. "Are they wearing *body suits*?!"

"I think they're something else entirely. I don't think they're people," Bunson answered grimly, loading a truncheon into his hand. Then, to the rest of the barricade team, he shouted, "Look alive everybody! We've got incoming!"

Verboga pressed their helmet com again and gave an order to fire a round of suppressants against the approaching wall. The tactical force shot off bean bag rounds, tagging quorbins. Some were knocked off their feet, but rapidly stood and resumed the charge. A few took hits that split their rinds, falling and oozing cream only to disappear under the feet of their comrades.

"They're not people," Bunson muttered as he watched them close in. He shouted one more time, "Hand-to-hand! Hand-to-hand!"

And then the quorbin smashed into the line.

LAZY NATIONS and Shelly Weedler approached the ring of law enforcement vehicles just as the gas projectiles were fired into the Castle of the Moon. The two women stayed low and kept quiet, and given the expectation that the entire area was shielded from the outside world, none of the assembled units paid attention to anything but the target.

Lazy and Shelly remained completely unobserved as the events of the skirmish unfolded.

For her part, Lazy Nations was intently studying the face of the building prior to the initial volley, and her brow only furrowed more intensely as the gas attack was executed. It was a difficult proposition to unpack exactly how they were going to get into the hotel and make sure the werewolves inside *weren't* murdered.

When they caught sight of The Ankh amidst the tendrils of chemicals emerging from the building, the urgency only accelerated. Both Shelly and Lazy tracked the superhero's approach until the last flip of their cape disappeared into the fog of the building. Shelly grabbed Lazy's upper arm and gave her a pleading, desperate look.

Lazy glanced around, fervently trying to figure out how to get into the building in front of all these armored cops in order to stop a superhero from murdering a pair of werewolves.

And that was when the quorbin rushed out of the hotel.

The kinetic heat of the oncoming brawl vibrated through Lazy, even in the relative chill of the evening. She swept Shelly behind her with one arm, then raised her fists to get ready to scrap.

They weren't directly in the path of the quorbin rush, but a few of the creatures spotted Lazy and detoured toward her. Now that they were less shocking, she was able to rapidly drop them. She used her fists to push one back and then flattened its head by slamming them both together around it. She cut the legs out from under another with a deft foot sweep before using her knees to erupt its chest. She transferred the momentum of a third to launch it into the air and impale it on a parking meter.

"Holy shit, girl," Shelly said in awe. "You are a fucking machine."

Lazy Nations looked at Shelly Weedler without affectation and shrugged.

Then she waded into the mix of quorbin and police, pulling gas masks off the unconscious forms of a pair of battered officers. She waited a moment, watching, and nodded in approval when she saw their chests rising and falling. They were knocked out cold, but still breathing. She adjusted one of the masks over her face and handed the other to Shelly.

"Okay, wow. Here we go," Shelly said under her breath as she took the mask proffered by Lazy. She strapped the mask on awkwardly and lined up behind her companion, doing her best to assume a similarly coiled stance.

Without warning, Lazy Nations sprinted toward the hotel, compact and forceful in her motion. Shelly Weedler lunged after her, pressing herself to keep pace.

INSIDE THE CASTLE of the Moon, The Ankh had wrought devastation against the quorbin that had tried to stop the superhero. The room stank with the sloppy remains of the monsters.

Covered in stains and sludge now, The Ankh stood at the

bottom of the stairs, peering up at the pair of werewolves on the elegant landing. The Ankh's belt was empty of silver spikes, nearly all of them spent in the bodies of the quorbin littering the wide lobby and forming a grotesque trail to the stairs. Only two spikes remained, one in each hand of The Ankh.

"PESTILENT DEMONS!" The Ankh declared, "YOUR FOUL PRESENCE IN THIS PLACE AND IN THIS CITY IS AT AN END! PREPARE TO BE DESTROYED BY THE TRUE CHAMPION OF THE MOON! I AM...THE ANKH!!"

Romana hissed and flung her arms out, her brutal claws spread and ready. Erskine roared and leapt down the stairs toward The Ankh.

The Ankh sprang into action, leaping up the stairs five at a time.

As the two met, The Ankh vaulted off of Erskine's meaty frame and propelled further up the stairs, clashing with Romana as they achieved the landing. Erskine tumbled down the staircase, then corrected and raced back upward to the landing.

The three whirled in a deadly dance as The Ankh's cape threw brilliant accent marks over the combat. Unbelievably, the werewolves seemed to be flagging. Even though The Ankh had fought through a room full of their thralls, and faced uneven odds, the superhero seemed to be *gaining* in strength as the unholy beasts across from The Ankh tired, ebbing vitality.

The Ankh kicked Erskine in the chest, hard, and the werewolf fell to his knees. To the other side, The Ankh swept Romana's legs, forcing her into an unintentional cart-wheel that landed her on her back, legs shooting out.

"YOU END NOW, BEASTS!" declared The Ankh,

cutting an imposing figure with spikes raised to either side, above each werewolf.

Romana, dazed and watching her doom from what felt like a hundred yards away, reached out in her mind to what she thought was her benefactor, the gift-giver that had yielded the Castle of the Moon to her, that stronghold she had been building to render unto her master.

Her mind filled with the perfect circle of Mr. Moon's head. He blinked. And the devil smiled broadly at her.

"Urgh!" Lazy Nations grunted as she tackled The Ankh.

"VILLAIN! WHY DO YOU STAND IN THE WAY OF JUSTICE!" yelled The Ankh, as they shook off Lazy Nations and struggled to their feet.

"No, you fucking asshole!" yelled Shelly Weedler from the bottom of the lobby staircase. "If you kill the werewolves, it is going to seriously fuck things up! Seriously!! Like, don't do it you fucking clown!"

"YOU CANNOT PERCEIVE THE MACHINE OF JUSTICE WITH THE CLARITY THAT IS POSSESSED BY I– THE ANKH– SHELLY WEEDLER!" roared The Ankh.

The werewolves were beginning to push themselves up in an effort to stand once again.

Lazy Nations rolled to one side and prepared to take another charge at subduing The Ankh.

Shelly Weedler couldn't conceive of how she could help, but it didn't stop her from sprinting toward the landing.

"KING OF DIAMONDS ON TARGET," Captain Hart reported from his F-600 Hellshrike as it screamed toward the Hotel Richmond.

"Queen of Hearts on target," Captain Boner returned as her F-600 Hellshrike complemented Hart's trajectory.

"Enemy sent ground forces at us," came the response from the SRDF vehicle situated with the tactical units below. "But shouldn't impede us from making the incursion. Prepare to subdue the werewolves and retrieve the robot."

A brief pause, then: "Knock on the door, knock it out."

"Copy," replied Captain Boner.

"Copy," replied Captain Hart.

The pilots each flipped open their firing controls, and in sync, fired their EMP missiles into the face of the Hotel Richmond. They wouldn't cause harm to anything living, but they would disable an electronic entity completely, even one of an extra-planetary origin.

The missiles found their target as the pilots streaked their jets over the top of the Hotel Richmond.

EVERYTHING SEEMED to shift into slow motion as Lazy Nations turned toward the front of the hotel and saw the incoming missiles. Two of them. She powered herself off the stairs, shouldered The Ankh to one side before they could impale Romana with one of their spikes, and leapt down the flight below her to the foot of the stairs, where she grabbed Shelly and pulled her low to cover.

The missiles didn't explode.

And the fact that they didn't issue a concussive force gave Lazy Nations a moment to appreciate the picture around the landing.

One of the missiles had embedded itself below the gallery floor, sparking where it had settled. The other missile had followed a higher arching path. It had landed in the elevator bank three floors up. On its way, it had blown through a chain suspending a beautiful ornate chandelier hanging over the plush, crimson carpeting of the landing. The werewolves looked up as it fell, each of them standing perfectly within its circumference.

The silver chandelier pierced Romana and Erskine, impaling them each to the landing of the Castle of the Moon. Ichor sprayed from them both as they withered and fumed, their bodies pinned.

"Nooooooo!!" Shelly screamed.

The timed EMP pulses of the missiles erupted, throwing radiating waves across the open area of the hotel and cutting off all the lights in its wake.

In the darkness, reality shifted wildly.

45

Half an hour earlier, Marcy Egg, sitting behind the desk at the Royal Leisure Motor Inn, was getting an earful from the owner of the establishment, Mr. Jeffords.

Mr. Jeffords had driven by earlier in the evening and was absolutely appalled by the state of the building, specifically what seemed to be growth and discoloration on the exterior of room six, as well as the pulsing purple light emanating from it. It was visible from the street, and what the Royal Leisure Motor Inn did *not* need was another reason for patrons to avoid it, after all that horrible rash business.

Marcy had explained that the room was paid in full, and that was a big deal, because business hadn't been so good lately, what with the overblown rumors of the motel being responsible for transmitting that rash and all. But if it was an issue with some kind of lights thing, of course Marcy would go get them to turn it off, because that was against the rules. It was new, though, and must have not been that bad, because it wasn't noticeable from the office.

She hung up the phone, and looked out the side

window of the office. The door of number six was now festooned with odd plant growth that snaked out onto the building and over the doors and windows of adjacent rooms. A constant, high-intensity light cascaded across her face, oscillating between a deep purple and striking violet light.

Maybe it was a bit noticeable. Marcy harrumphed, and slipped into the back room to dip her hand into a bag of keys, all the same, and all able to open any door anywhere across the motel. She slipped about twenty keys onto a giant metal ring and clipped the metal ring to a belt loop, where it would lend a sense of gravity and authority, and where she could jangle it for emphasis. There was something about having a lot of keys on one's person that just gave the impression that you were important and didn't have the time to be delayed or trifled with.

Keys on her hip, she left the office and crossed the parking lot, fighting back the urge to stall by picking up a few stray candy bar wrappers.

She hitched up her shorts as she arrived at the door to number six and noted the sweet tang in the air from the vines stuck to the building. The aroma was floral, but also a little bit sickening. There was an almost meaty undertone to the scent.

She knocked, one rap and then a quick double-tap of the knuckles. She heard someone moving inside the room, the familiar sound of someone sliding off the vaguely plasticky comforter on a bed to pad the few feet to the door.

Right at that moment, across town, Romana and Erskine were pinned to the opulent landing of the Hotel Richmond/Castle of the Moon by an elegant silver chandelier, where they expired.

In a mountainside clearing, four out of five small, worn

stones faintly glowed a halo of pale yellow. Only one remained dull and unlit.

The door of number six opened.

It wasn't quite an explosion, in that there was no flame and no destruction, but the force of the shift in the nature of being was concussive, and it struck Marcy Egg full in the chest.

She really didn't have any chance to figure out what was going on. Or what was happening to her.

Marcy had the briefest glimpse into the interior of number six, which seemed to be a menagerie of flora and fauna and the fantastic. There seemed to be, where the bathroom should have been, a giant hole in the floor, into which flowed giant roots and stalks. Marcy blinked and thought she saw an alligator's head peeking up out of the hole, laying its long snout casually and blissfully across the motel room floor. Was there a tattered monkey sitting on the opposite side of the hole? A pair of human legs in a skirt, crossed and sitting in the uncomfortable little chair next to the small round table with the phone? The same legs she had seen cross the parking lot?

All of that was just an impression, though. The experience she was having was one of being knocked, hard, by the shift in things. And she was sailing. Upward. The receding world was framed below her by her worn tennis shoes.

She could see the doorway become a small rectangle and shrink away from her. The rooftop and parking lot of the Royal Leisure Motor Inn. The area around the motel along the service road, next to the highway. The city itself. The web of lights across the ground from a distance, the view she would get if she were returning to the city at night in an airplane. A bank of clouds. And then the upper atmosphere.

Marcy Egg banged her elbow on a satellite, painfully, and as she continued away from the earth, rubbing it to speed through the feeling, somewhere a teen's download was interrupted.

Then the whole of the Earth was between her tennis shoes, a breathtaking firsthand sight normally reserved for astronauts or the super rich.

She whizzed by the moon and into space, cruising through the asteroid belt and onward to the outer planets.

Whatever was behind that door really blew her off her feet, and it didn't seem like it was going to be stopping any time soon.

46
_____

S helly Weedler and Lazy Nations regained consciousness at about the same time, returning to awareness to find that their bodies had been standing and facing one another across the curved staircase. The first thing they saw was each others' eyes– apparently their gazes had been locked for an indeterminate amount of time since the werewolves died, and they only just achieved the wherewithal to have any realization of it.

The room was no longer plunged into darkness, although there wasn't an obvious light source for the swimmy ambient mauve illumination suffusing it. Clumps of haze drifted and spiraled around the large lobby room.

"Fuuuuuuuuuuuuuuuuuuuck," Shelly exhaled. "Well, that didn't go as planned. I guess we didn't manage to stop..." She paused and swung a glance over to where The Ankh had been. Lazy Nations followed Shelly's gaze.

A mound made of bandages, trunks, boots, cape and a visor sat piled where the superhero had last stood. Cheesy goo spurted from the pile intermittently in a fountain. MISSION ACCOMPLISHED.

"Ugh," Shelly said.

Lazy Nations kicked a foot against the opulent carpet of the landing, and shrugged her shoulders. "That's it. Everything is weirder now. Let's hope your dog friend has a trick up it's...uh...sleeve before the last one of these werewolves bites it."

"Yeah..." Shelly replied, not sounding very confident, given how things had happened so far. A random soap bubble, a foot in diameter, floated behind her and popped. She flinched slightly at the cartoonish popping noise, and then continued. "How weird do you think things are going to be? How bad do you think it's gotten?"

They headed down the stairs together. Everywhere a human body had lain, rendered unconscious by the knockout gas, was a cut rate action figure, the kind that you might buy at a dollar store that tried to imply an association with an intellectual property.

"Pretty bad. Pretty weird," Lazy Nations responded. She gently nudged a figure out of their walking path with the toe of her shoe. It had a diamond-shaped USA shield, its body was painted with a webbing pattern over red and blue coloration, and it wore a cape with a bat on it.

Both Shelly and Lazy snapped their heads up as a pair of shapes sprang through the front door of the hotel.

They were puppets.

"Freeze!" yelled one.

"Hands up and stay right there!" joined the other.

Each had an oversized plush gun in their hands, which were propped up by puppeteering sticks.

"Fuck, I'm never going to get used to any of this," Shelly muttered.

The puppets approached them, moving in the way that puppets do to imply that running is happening: lots of bouncing up and down in place, with some ostentatious side-to-side waggling, while the actual advancement is accomplished by a smooth glide along the axis of motion. The legs of the puppets just dangled beneath them.

"Where's the robot! Where's the dog!" demanded Bunson.

"The EMP should have knocked it out– the robot– and then it's just about catching a dog, although that can be tough, the dog might just think we're playing around, that's what happens a lot of times," Mandel explained, their puppet form flopping its head comically around as they looked for Zappazmazoid and Biscuit.

"The robot? The dog??" Shelly exploded. "You! You! You! Child education-looking cretins! The dog and the robot are trying to STOP this from happening! It's the werewolves! The werewolves did this! But! But! But we have to keep the werewolves alive! The more werewolves die, the more Mr. Moon changes reality from particle to wave and then we get shit like this! So it's Mr. Moon! Mr. Moon is the problem! And there's only one– one fucking– werewolf left! That one dies and who knows what this is! We're all just living in a dream then? Like, forever?! I don't want to go back to high school and have to shit in my locker and get graded on it or whatever– repeatedly!"

The puppets looked at Shelly with an expression of flat consternation that only puppets can muster.

"But we were told it was the robot and the dog..." Mandel began to respond, though without much confidence.

"BY WHO!? By whom?! Who by?! *I*," Shelly continued, really emphasizing the "I" when she got to it, "TALKED to the robot. And the dog I guess, but the dog didn't talk. The dog probably talks now. I got the straight story. The *robot* is the, whatever, the good guy here. And you are the bad people or the tools of the bad people. Or, that's probably too reductive really. Your people undoubtedly mean well, but they do not have the full story or are dumb or scared or whatever makes people do bad things. ARGH!"

For her part, Lazy Nations just watched the conversation, and subtly, carefully, just made sure that there weren't any action figures underfoot.

"Okay," Bunson acknowledged, then turned to Mandel. "Let's get the tactical forces in here to do a sweep, but this feels like information we should get to Hart and Boner. Sounds like there's more to the picture than maybe they know."

"Do ya think?" Shelly interrupted. She sized up the two puppets. The fact that they were puppets made her wonder if maybe she was being too hard on them. As she looked down to their feet, Shelly looked through a sliver in perception, and experienced a wild wave of vertigo as she met the desperate eyes of the human forms of Bunson and Mandel, operating their puppet forms from...somewhere. Shelly stumbled a little and grabbed her forehead. The puppets shook their arms and gave a cute little yell.

"Are you OK?" Lazy asked Shelly, offering a hand to steady her.

"Yeah, yeah," Shelly answered quietly. "Just a wave."

THE QUARTET STEPPED OUTSIDE, where they found that a similar quality of ambiguously illuminated violet light pervaded the atmosphere. The buildings of the skyline danced and swayed with or against the night breeze in no discernible pattern.

All around them, the tactical forces were a mix of human-sized wind-up toys and blocky wooden robots. The vehicles were a pell-mell of oversized child toys and inexplicable, giant random objects with wheels stuck on. A few feet away sat a tuna can the size of a tank with four tires stuck to the outer perimeter of it.

"Look, we have some things to deal with here," Bunson admitted to Shelly and Lazy in a massive display of understatement. "Can you just hang tight while we figure some things out?"

"Like how to drive that thing," Mandel interjected, waving a noodly arm at the tuna can with tires.

"And then when we sort out some basics," Bunson continued, "the two of you can come down to the station and help us augment our understanding of what exactly in the hell is going on here. And maybe what we can actually do about it all."

"Sure, sure," Shelly replied. To her surprise, she found that one of those blankets was already draped over her shoulders, again. She wasn't quite sure where it had come from.

"Great, then, hang tight," Bunson repeated. "We'll get back to you within thirty and get moving. Take a load off if you can find a place to sit down here."

The puppets flounced away to try to piece together a plan with their collected toybox forces.

"C'mon," Lazy Nations said as soon as they were out of sight. "Let's get out of here."

"What?" Shelly asked, baffled.

"You and me. Let's get out of here," Lazy said. "These people have at best only stood around while the real action was happening, and, at worst, genuinely helped fuck things up. We don't want to be stuck with them. We won't get anything done. We need to find your dog and your robot. They're the ones that know what's going on, pretty obviously, based on how things went when those two werewolves got spiked. And if we are sitting around with these cops– and whoever their friends are– either we're not going to see the dog and the robot at all, or if we do, they're going to be put in some kind of spin cycle because somebody has a point of pride to protect about being in pursuit of the dog and the robot in the first place. It's a dead end, being with these people."

Shelly realized that the blanket that had been across her shoulders was gone.

"Besides," Lazy Nations added, strolling sideways to leave the perimeter of fun house vehicles. "I think with the way things are, it's going to be really easy to just walk away."

47

Captains Hart and Boner each received a confirmation ping on their dashboards when their EMP missiles released their pulses, and each smiled in anticipation of the impending capture of the extraplanetary target.

Second later, however, they were slammed back into their control seats as if they'd been hit with a sudden g-force shock. Captain Hart blacked out for a few seconds. Captain Boner felt tears stream from her eyes.

As the shock passed, and they felt their bodies regain their expected state, it became obvious that the rest of the world had not.

The night sky they flew their jets through was no longer black dotted with pinpoints of stars. Instead it was a rich burgundy, streaking to hazy purples and violets. The stars had rearranged, and looked as if they were drawn by hand. Some were simple scribbles of yellow, while others were ornate stacks of pinwheels, composed of different textures and colors, rotating against one another in complex cycles.

Connecting the stars were pale lines, sketching constellations, and between the lines were virtually transparent panes of what looked like stained glass, so that each constellation demonstrated precisely what it represented as a living thing. The stars quivered and rotated as the bodies moved and reacted to one another across the newly rich color of space. Only the waxing moon remained untouched by the change.

"Do you see..." Captain Hart asked.

"Yes," affirmed Captain Boner. "If we're both seeing it, psychic attack?"

"That seems the most likely scenario to me," agreed Hart. "Engaging shi-kay-doh meditation technique."

"Copy," responded Boner.

The two pilots began breathing deeply, allowing their jets to cruise at a steady, automatic trajectory. They stretched out their hands across the dashboards of their respective cockpits and splayed their fingers, rolling the focus of their minds between the troughs inside each pair of knuckles in order.

"Guh-haw!" guffawed a constellation that looked like an anthropomorphized animal from an early twentieth century cartoon, complete with patchwork trousers held up by buttoned suspenders and a silly little hat. "That's not what it is! Nossir!"

The pilots maintained their breathing and focus discipline.

"Look fellers," the constellation addressed them, its head growing larger to fill up their swathe of the sky. It remained two-dimensional, so that the impression was less one of an actual approach as much as it being stretched to the corners of their field of view at a shocking speed.

"Things are different now!" the constellation continued, as a crab constellation with a handlebar mustache threw up pinchers in agreement. "And, I think, guh-haw!, for the better! Look at yourselves, so many rules, so much panic over how things oughta be. That's not the way we're headed, nossir, we're headed for the 'right' way, for things to be just to be whatever flows, whatever that may be. The dam's almost broken, fellers, and the river's going to flow! I think one of you made sure the farmer is just a head now, and the hen house almost entirely a fox house, and I! Fer one! Think that's much more fun!"

Hart and Boner realized that they were no longer within their cockpits, but rather sitting astride two massive birds composed entirely of blood. The hands that they had spread across their dashboards were spread across the necks of the literal blood shrikes, and they could tell intuitively that the contact was enough to compel the gargantuan animals to do precisely what they wanted them to do.

Stunned, Hart and Boner looked over at each other, and then down, watching as the birds perched in the stained glass palm of the constellation's hand. Just as quickly, the constellation dropped its hand out from underneath them, giving the impression of moving through dimensional space by shrinking and reorienting its shape in jags away from them.

The birds immediately spread their wings and hovered, facing the vision before them.

It tipped its cap and opened one eye very wide. "Whelp! I have to shake a leg! Hope to see ya again, real soon! Guh-haw!"

The cartoon constellation recessed into the sky, jaunting along, heels clicking occasionally in its merry retreat into deeper space. Its compatriots bounced and shimmied as it sang along its way.

A-buh-beh-buh-bee!

Ah'm a-swimmin' on tha wine dark sea!

That, a-beh-buh-bee,

Does suit me!

48

The Royal Leisure Motor Inn had also seen an abrupt and monumental transformation– the magnitude of which was enough to have flung Marcy Egg on an endless trajectory through space.

The walls of the motel, the edifice itself, had been replaced with the giant form of Wyatt the lab assistant curled in the bygone shape of the building, as if the image had been cut out of the pages of D'Aulaire's Mythology. Where the office had been was Wyatt's titanic head, his form curling around where the parking lot had lain, with doors to each of the rooms metered out along his body. Number six sat directly at his groin. Creeping vines festooned the entirety of the area, sewing the gargantuan shape to the earth and snaking above him to create layered towers of canopies. Animals and other more fantastic creatures crawled across the surface and passed in and out of door-ways to create a tableau worthy of Hieronymous Bosch.

Above them all bloomed a thick stalk, rising from Wyatt's midsection, a massive leaf curling from it to form a platform. On that, the Queen held court, sitting in a topiary throne, surrounded by her beastly and vegetative courtesans. Hypnotically beautiful and horrid at once, her fronds stretched out into feathery plumes, anchored by pulsing vines, knotted like intestines, all of which sat on top of Gloria's long, firm legs, coquettishly crossed in front of her on the throne.

The menagerie paraded and pranced in front of her, scuttling and squirming over the fallen form of the erstwhile lab assistant in a sickening, decadent cabaret act.

The queen grew her new garden at the Royal Leisure Motor Inn, and awaited her king, awaited the arrival of Mr. Moon, awaited the permanent ushering in of the new way that let her live and thrive as she was.

49

After Shelly Weedler and Lazy Nations left the Hotel Richmond, they decided to return to Shelly's apartment. It was as good a place as any to gather themselves and try to come up with an idea of what to do next, or where to go next, and Shelly had a bit more of a sense of hospitality and invitation to her general mental makeup. Lazy would have been unperturbed to have Shelly over to her apartment, but Lazy wouldn't necessarily think to issue the invitation out loud, and would not have considered making a guest comfortable once they arrived. Shelly would; it was implicitly obvious that she was just better at all that stuff.

The walk was disconcerting in terms of what they saw, and how it all felt, the experience of walking over the distance and how the distance complied, accordioning itself so that what should have been a couple miles took seconds and what should have been fifty feet took more than an hour to traverse.

Shelly lifted her key to the outside door of the foyer to

her building and it slid into the lock. The lock cooed in response, in an encouraging, passionate way, as if to reassure the key it was really doing a good job and should keep going. The foyer door opened, and Shelly's key went limp in her hand. Somehow she could tell it felt inadequate and ashamed at needing to be coddled so much by the exterior lock. The interior lock took pity on all of them, and the door to the apartment stairs just swung open, as if it were trying to get out of the way. By the time Shelly and Lazy reached Shelly's floor, it felt like they were on a treadmill or moving walkway that was operating at such a speed that it was flinging them along inexorably. The two braced themselves, sure that they were going to be smashed into the apartment door, but then they were inside, standing in the entry area to the apartment without having had to open the door at all.

"Hello? Shelly? Are you home?" a voice called to them from further inside the apartment.

"Ye-es?" answered Shelly, confused at not recognizing the voice in her own home. She shot her eyes to Lazy Nations, and then stepped further in, past the front window, around the dining room table, and into the living room behind the couch. Lazy Nations followed her, keeping pace but coiled with readiness to shove Shelly aside and step in front of her if the need arose.

"Hi there, welcome home," said Biscuit as the two women turned the corner. Shelly and Lazy's mouths fell fully open. They had seen a lot that evening, but somehow, this was the most surprising of all.

Biscuit sat in the maroon easy chair just inside the living room. The chocolate lab's legs were crossed, casually, as it rocked slightly in the chair. In one of his forepaws, he had a bottle of Major Stoneway Lager, a beer from the six pack Shelly kept in the fridge in case anyone came over and answered "beer" to the question "do you want something to drink?"

Biscuit had an intelligent look on his face, and his tongue hung out of his open, panting mouth. He was wearing a necktie and a shirt collar with it, although no shirt. Zappazmazoid's head, rather than being attached to Biscuit's, was hanging suspended in air beside the dog, as if held in an invisible thought balloon.

"I can talk now, as you observe," Biscuit acknowledged, and then apologetically added, "I hope it's okay I grabbed a beer. I just wanted to take a little bit of the edge off. It's been a pretty weird night. All around, but, you know, for me specifically too. As in, I can talk now, and I have the cognition that comes with speech as well. Which is all pretty new to me, as you may be able to imagine."

The dog took a long pull on the beer, and then let his mouth fall back open and tongue roll out to its full length again.

"Sure, sure that's...fine," Shelly struggled to respond. "The beer, it's really for guests anyway, so..."

Zappazmazoid interrupted, "Time is against us! Only one pillar of the gate remains. We failed to locate and return the escaped entity to its prison before the destruction of the penultimate two pillars, and the challenge has gotten more difficult and severe as a result."

"We tried to stop that superhero from killing the werewolves," Shelly began to explain. "But then somebody shot these electronic missiles into the hotel, and a chandelier impaled the werewolves and..."

"Ah– I do not mean to imply that you have failed in some task to which you were obligated, Shelly Weedler," Zappazmazoid said. "Truly, this is my task, and my partner here has agreed to assist me in the mission. Everything you have endeavored to do up to this point, along with your friend, is above and beyond, and your world and species should be grateful that you have made the effort. Even if the result is not what we had hoped. Yet!"

"Uh-huh, okay," Shelly said, not entirely accepting the sentiment.

"Hello, I am Zappazmazoid," said Zappazmazoid to Lazy Nations, realizing that a formal greeting had yet to be made.

"Oh, yeah," Lazy Nations responded. "I'm Lazy. Lazy Nations. Good...to meet you. Shelly told me about you. We were all interested in the same book. You got it, though." And then, having reminded herself of the book and her sister's recommendation, Lazy muttered, "Hm. I have to call my sister and see if she's all right. And I have to call my dad. He's going to be weird about it if he, like, got turned into something."

"And I'm Biscuit," Biscuit piped up, butting into the introduction. "I can talk now, but I couldn't until earlier this evening. Aaaaaand, I gotta take a leak. I see it's down the hall, right?"

"Um, yeah," Shelly answered.

Biscuit put his beer on the side table, strolled down the hall, popped the toilet seat up, and began to urinate, standing on his hind legs, into the toilet without closing the door. He braced himself with one of his fore paws resting against the wall above the toilet.

Shelly tracked it all in a sort of hypnotized fascination, from the click-click-click of Biscuit's back paws advancing down the hall to the dog peeing like a man in full view of the rest of the group like a shameless college boyfriend, until she was finally able to tear her eyes away and look back at Zappazmazoid.

Lazy Nations took advantage of the moment to step

aside and place a phone call, either to her sister or father. Shelly could hear her whispering from the dining room, "Okay, great – you're all right? Yes, everything *has* gotten pretty weird..."

"So," Shelly mustered up her courage. "So...what do we do now?"

"Now?" Zappazmazoid mused, floating in a tiny circle as if buoyed by a pool of invisible water. "Biscuit and I still have the book which is the device to imprison the entity and push it back into its prison. It has not been clear where the entity may be sequestered, but with one pillar remaining, I believe it is likely that it will not be able to resist making a show, a ritual of crushing that final pillar in a celebration of locking in its desired quality of reality. The danger will be great, but I believe our greatest chance of subverting its wishes will be to interrupt this ritual, prevent the demise of the werewolf that is the last pillar, and send the entity back to its prison. We should endeavor to do this, and if we fail, we will be there to fall so that we do not have to live in the further nightmare of an unruly existence."

"I don't like the sound of that," Shelly Weedler reflected, "but I suppose you're right. This does seem like a give-it-our-all-or-go-down-fighting kind of situation."

She glanced back into the dining room where Lazy Nations spoke in a hushed tone of concern, twisting her hair absent-mindedly.

"I'm glad I'm friends with her now, though– that makes me feel like we've got a little more of a shot," Shelly said.

"What's that?" Biscuit asked as he returned from down the hall. He picked his beer back up, and dropped back into the easy chair.

"Her. Lazy. I was just saying I'm glad she's here and I'm glad I know her. Especially right now."

"Why?" Biscuit prompted.

"Well," Shelly said, "From what I've seen so far, she is just always ready to fucking kick some ass."

"Mmm," Biscuit said, taking a swing of his beer. "Man, Lager is great, right?"

50

Bunson and Mandel stood with their arms stretched out from their puppet bodies. They quivered and shook, and their puppet heads rolled side-to-side in an exaggerated show of overwhelmed dismay.

"We lost them!! How could we looooooose them! Did anyone see where they went?! Anyone?!" Mandel flung their puppet arms over their head and again shook them like twin noodles. "We're going to count to ten, and when we get to ten, they better Be! Right! Here!"

"One!"

"Two!"

"Three!"

"Four!"

"Five!"

"Six!"

The puppet officers had been alternating numbers, but now synchronized and finished the count in unison.

"Seven!"

"Eight!"

"Nine!"

"Oohhhhhh no! We're almost there!" said Bunson.

"They're not here and we're going to get all the way to..." Mandel paused dramatically.

"Ten! AAAAAAAAAAAggggghh!!" shouted the puppets, both of them throwing their arms over their heads and bouncing up and down as they criss-crossed each another within the confines of a small circle of panic. "How! Could! We! Looooooooose! Them!"

51

D r. Martina Desmond had begun to feel like a prison warden even before the plants held in the facility below started to sing their mournful song.

She was the only one that had shown herself to be unaffected by the particulate they released, perhaps because she had been there for their maturation and evolution. Every other researcher, maybe with the exception of the missing Wyatt, rapidly succumbed to illness and incapacitation, even without the horrifying dosage that had killed that poor girl outside the original garden.

The plants yearned to return to their queen, and now battered their bodies against the walls of the facility, humming and raising their voices in pleading desire.

Dr. Desmond felt forgotten in her desolation, as if she had been hurled into her own Tartarus for her sins, chained to an invisible rock with only the chorus of her damned progeny to keep her company.

She wondered if anyone would remember her, if anyone would come to retrieve her and return her to the land of the living.

52

"Oh no, I'm fine. Thank you for calling, though, I really appreciate the consideration," replied the young man into the receiver. He sat cross-legged, hovering about two and a half feet off the floor of his simple apartment. The modest collection of his possessions orbited him in slow, drifting ellipses.

"This is all fairly unusual to my experience of living so far, of course," he admitted without judgment. "But I have figured that any effort to debate reality is really going to be a losing proposition. If reality changes and you try to assert that it has not changed, then, in all deference to our sister, you are actually the crazy one."

"Mm-hm," replied to the voice on the other side of the phone.

"Speaking of, have you called her and dad as well? Good, I'm sure they appreciated the check-in. Yes, I do expect that our family, of all people, are managing to cope better than most in our own particular ways.

"Now, I have not had the time to process this fully, so, I may be speaking from a bit of a shallowly reactive place, but listening to what you have said here, maybe you would deign to listen to some thoughts from me on the matter, which, yes, could be taken as advice if you were so inclined.

"Mm-hm. Okay. Good. Thank you for humoring me.

"As we have agreed, the substantive experience of living in this world or universe or however you may want to couch the context has changed, it's safe to say, dramatically. I think that it is also fair to say, and I do not mean this as a critique, just an acknowledgment, that your approach to solving problems has traditionally manifested as a physical act.

"Oh, I'm not trying to protect your feelings, I'm just trying to be fair and sketch out the picture in terms that makes sense to both of us, so that we can take a deeper dive on what the implications, now, may be.

"Good. I apologize, I don't mean to belabor the point, just set the starting point." Gnarly Nations rolled his eyes upward and to the left, visualizing his thesis.

"Just because the nature of what is physical seems to have changed, I don't think that indicates that you should change the way you are or how you do things. That's you, and I love you for it. I think you're a good person who genuinely tries to help whenever the opportunity arises. I am simply suggesting that what constitutes physical now does not align with historical behavior."

Gnarly tracked his toaster oven as it bumped along several feet from him, drifting into his point of view from the left and continuing on across his field of vision to the right.

"But what I am suggesting is that how you apply that approach may change, and it could be worthwhile to loosen your expectations while still attending to things as you would otherwise do. That is, with everything being different, consider that you may be able to do things now that accomplish your objectives that would have been impossible before this, and allow for the benefit of that, rather than being frustrated and shattering yourself against not being able to do some things that you have always known the ability to achieve.

"Yes, it's a bit of a jumble of a thought, but just consider it."

"OK, good luck. I love you. Yes, I love you too. You're a terrific sister."

Gnarly hung up the phone, closed his eyes, opened his mouth, and a spoon of rice broke from the orbit and delivered itself to him, then zipped off to chase the plastic container from which it could refill.

He chewed and then sighed, allowing a warm sense of awareness to extend to the edges of his apartment. Gnarly Nations felt nuclear, with the various objects floating around him his mitochondrial brethren.

53

S ince the business with the werewolf attack, Maximum Burrito number one five four at 2407 Chestnut Avenue had, understandably, been closed for business. It was an inconvenience for some of the regulars, but considering what had gone on, they understood why that was the case.

As their shift began, however, Elvin and Darcy, neither of whom had spoken with the other since the attack, as they were very different people outside of work and their connection was strictly professional, found themselves approaching the doorstep of their restaurant. They were drawn there. It felt like the place they needed to be.

As they approached from opposite diagonals to the front of the restaurant, they became aware of one another without directly looking at each other. Instead they observed the face of the establishment, which was utterly colorless. It stood in shades of gray, like a photograph in the back pages of a very old newspaper, and equally dimensionless.

Arriving at the door, Darcy held it open for Elvin, and he stepped inside. As they both crossed the threshold, desaturated color bled from the door across the facade, deepening and brightening each moment. The face of the Maximum Burrito seemed to protrude into three dimensional space, like a hand opening to offer itself in friendship.

Darcy and Elvin stepped behind the counter, dropped on their aprons and faced each other. They flowed together, a blinding white light, an ouroboros of perfect cooperation and synchronicity.

The Maximum Burrito was open again, and staffing it was a single being composed of two individuals living as a testament to the possibility of perfect harmony between separate identities working toward a shared goal.

If one were to truly stare into the ball of luminescence, they might be able to make out the distinct action of two bodies working together as a frictionless machine, but there would be a legitimate risk of going blind at the sight of real perfection. And, considering what the union produced, no one who passed through the line at the newly restored Maximum Burrito thought to pursue such an invasive inspection.

The line immediately began to assemble and snaked across the city, criss-crossing it over and over. Almost anywhere anyone went, they ran into a section of the line to the Maximum Burrito, as if it were a circulatory system embedded into the tissue of the city. At the same time, anyone intending to get in the queue for the restaurant easily found the end of the line and was subsequently served with absolute efficiency and accuracy.

Online reviews were perfect too; five out of five stars.

54

Rod Lorenzen sat behind the desk at the city morgue. He had taken a little time off after the pair of legs had gotten up by themselves and left, but it turned out he felt more creeped out being at home than working overnight at the morgue. Rod thought of it like this: if there are just sets of legs walking around out there, he'd rather run into them at work, where it was somebody else's space, than at home, which was his personal space. He really didn't like the idea of running into a pair of legs walking around in a place he thought of as his own.

Rod had been behind his wooden desk, churning his way through the very same copy of the magazine SMASH!: Music for Everybody, when the third and fourth pillar of the gate had fallen. He had been behind the desk ever since, staring at the wall of drawers. They were each lighting up with a brilliant color, one at a time, and blaring different tunes of different genres in turn. Rod, frozen, stared and listened.

Aquamarine.

Adult Morality Ballads.

Yooooooooouuuuuuu
You took it from me.
And
Iiiiiiiiiiiiiiiiiiiiiiiiii
Did not have it
To giiiiiiiiiiive
Iiiiiiiiiiiiiiiiiiiiiiiiiii
Am less than
Emp-ty
But yoooooooooooooouuuuuu
Are the one
In a
Graaaaaaaaaaaaaaaaave
Rod grimaced.
Hot salmon.
Acidgum Pop.
Baby, baby, baby,
You're drooling on my bottom
You're drooling on my back
Get back!
Don't worry,
I'm going to work you
I'm going to work your
Assssssssssssssssssssssssss-k
Me no questions,
I'll tell you no lies.
I'll just keep your big ears warm
With the inside of my thighs.

Rod was so thirsty. He didn't know the last time he'd had the opportunity to eat something or drink something or sleep for any amount of time. He felt like he was going to be found in 500 years, petrified like one of those sad trailer park mummies, and then his discoverers would lose it when they realized his eyes were still flicking around looking at the colored rectangles of the drawers and his ears were still working to hear the tunes erupting from within. Even if they were also probably weeping blood.

Rusty chartreuse.

Skunk Country.

They foooooound me,
Asleep in my truck again
They hooooooound me,
For running my mouth at them
I just wanna eat a steak
Give me a damn break
All I wanna do
Is eat a steak

"Gaaaaaaa–" groaned Rodrigo Lorenzen, his tongue lolling out of his foaming mouth.

55

Marcy Egg kept rocketing out into space, although she curiously didn't feel that much panic about it. It wasn't an unpleasant experience, truth be told, it was a bit like flopping onto a water bed and having the moment of contact last for an unbounded length of time.

The nature of her trajectory was such that she was set up to look backward along where she had already traveled, and she mostly did so, only occasionally looking from side-to-side to get the broader picture of where she had journeyed so far.

Space itself was populated with a panoply of stained-glass-bodied cartoon constellations, posturing in their places, interacting with a close neighbor, or swimming through the cosmos to find a new home.

Marcy sped by the little-known mascots of Real Buddies Mobile, the actual real buddies, Kip, Dick, and Rick. When she first saw them, they weren't acting very much like real buddies, they were wrestling with the intention to hurt one another, gouging each others' eyes, twisting each others' joints. Actually, Marcy was a little surprised she recognized them at all, but as she reflected on it, she thought it must be her crossword puzzles that let her know their names.

"Real Buddy that rhymes with what's in the basket they bring you for free at a Mexican restaurant."

"Not Nixon, but the 'tricky' Real Buddy."

"Real Buddy Lime ___ -ey."

How that let Marcy know what they looked like, she had zero idea, but that thought burbled deep beneath her conscious mind. She was more distracted by the debatable real buddy behavior in which they were engaged as they receded from her view, having moved from wrestling to furiously making out, doffing clothes so that constellations of dress shirts and pants floated away from the horny knotted bodies of the trio.

Time was extremely difficult to assess, and with the depth of space itself so highly mutable and possessed of no discernible landmarks, Marcy Egg gave up on trying to gauge it.

She watched what looked to be a tiny spacecraft whizz across the horizon of her chest. Then another, and another, until she felt that she had found herself resting next to a busy highway of interstellar commerce, even as she had the sense that her body continued its inexorable journey further and further away from the Earth.

Marcy observed with some interest, though no particular sentiment, as one of these craft deviated from the arc around her body and landed on her shirt. It dispensed a rover and a small crew of robots, and commenced construction on a series of buildings covering a patch of the right side of her stomach. After some stretch of time which involved the craft departing and returning a few times, the building was complete, a horseshoe-shaped structure with a flashing neon sign over one of its ends. It looked very much like the No / Vacancy sign at the motel, when it was working. This was a new building, though, everything should be in great working order, and extra clean.

At this thought, the alphanumeric character that Marcy thought would be the second "C" in the equivalent word "Vacancy" burned out, and would never light again.

The spacecraft that had brought the resources to build the edifice was joined by a puttering, sputtering, smaller rust-colored vehicle that belched little cigar-like smoke rings as it descended to Marcy's stomach. A bulbous, greenish creature emerged from it and strolled across the landing pad area to meet an insectoid in an official-looking, multi-legged coverall from the original ship.

Marcy could only judge the nature of their conversation by the way the sounds flowed between the two, but she did get the sense that the bulbous creature's flat, disinterested tones agitated and frustrated the officious clicking of the insectoid.

Finally, the insectoid and its robotic comrades reloaded onto the first craft, the insectoid made one last string of commands from the landing bridge of the ship, to which the bulbous creature simply shrugged, and then the spacecraft lifted off, the last activity visible the insectoid shaking its head and fuming as the bridge closed.

The bulbous creature slumped inside the structure, and the probably No / Vacancy sign sputtered in the void of space.

PERHAPS MARCY EGG had dozed off, or perhaps she hadn't, and nothing happened at all for some stretch of time.

Her attention was drawn back to existing with some sense of time right around the moment she noticed a third craft break from the occasional traffic arcing above her body and come to settle on her stomach outside the building on top of her.

An aperture opened in it and a crew of five humanoids exited it just in front of the office in which the bulbous alien resided. Four of the humanoids just looked human. The fifth looked like a frog person– human in general shape, but with a human-sized frog head. Although they all wore matching spacesuits, *its* boots and gloves had stylish web connections between the fingers and toes. To her surprise, it seemed as though the group was speaking English.

"What I am telling you," the foremost crewmember continued from a conversation begun within the ship, seemingly the leader or captain, "is that we all agreed. For everybody's comfort we are going to keep the ship at a very– VERY– reasonable 22 degrees. Whichever one of you clowns keeps cranking it up to 35 degrees, when I figure out *who* that is, you and me, we're going to have words. SO KNOCK IT OFF!"

The remaining members of the crew looked at their captain, and Marcy had the distinct feeling that the three other humans were looking out of the corner of their eyes at their amphibious colleague. The frog person blinked innocently.

Whether 22 or 35 degrees, that sounded pretty darn cold to Marcy and a lot to ask of an HVAC system to boot. But maybe temperature worked differently in space. Marcy had never dealt with temperature in space before.

"All right, I, for one, need to cool off, and I could use a night's sleep not cramped up in my bunk, and not sweating all over myself because someone can't keep their damn hands off the ship's thermostat. Let's see if we can get a couple rooms. Hastings, Bentwiddle, Gonzon, we can get you a cot probably and get you in one room. Croax, you're with me."

The collection of space travelers pushed into what seemed to be the office, and Marcy could see the resultant motion inside it. Mostly, that meant people standing around as terms were discussed and rooms were booked out, so it was the kind of minimal, bored transaction with which Marcy had a lot of experience.

It seemed that, in space, Marcy Egg didn't just work at the motel, she was the motel. It kind of reminded her of one of those "my wife" jokes, but she couldn't think of how it went. Probably for the better, really. That kind of stuff was a relic from a bygone age.

56

Captains Boner and Hart sat astride their Bloodshrikes, gliding through the mottled purple sky toward the landing strip of the home base of the Secret Rapid Defense Force.

The sky was crammed with odd bits and pieces of traffic in spurts. Their crimson trails crossed over the contrail of a commercial airline that seemed to be functioning normally, but as soon as it did, they were passed by a lanky individual sailing upward with a basketball held aloft overhead. The hooper was about to detonate the wildest dunk the world had ever seen, as soon as contact was made with a rim... although there was no rim in sight.

Then they passed a placid swathe where the only occupants of the sky were the two pilots and their bloody birds; space above and earth below equally remote from the lavender band of air they traversed.

As they closed in on their destination, Boner and Hart were passed by a stork carrying a baby nestled in a blanket, a precarious arrangement to see firsthand. Then they saw another, but *this* particular bird was absolutely going to town on a pickle as it flew. Slurping and nibbling and choking itself as it greedily mouthed the colossal gherkin, seemingly not making much headway in devouring it. The stork moved jerkily through the sky, at times flapping its wings madly, at times using them to grasp the pickle in a futile effort to have leverage against it.

The SRDF headquarters came into view, transformed from a massive but nondescript campus into a giant colosseum, ornately decorated and belching steam into the sky from minarets dotting its perimeter.

The Bloodshrikes seemed to know where to go, circling and then coasting down to land on a raised platform enclosed by the exterior border of the colosseum wall.

As they descended, the pilots saw a file cabinet sitting on the platform and giving the impression that it awaited their arrival. The birds landed in front of the file cabinet, side-by-side, allowing the pilots to dismount.

"The objective has experienced complications," the file cabinet said to the captains as their feet alighted onto the platform.

"Grís?" Captain Boner asked, cautious but already certain of the answer.

Captain Hart raised his eyebrows in surprise and took a slight, involuntary half-step backward. It was enough to give him a different angle onto Grís, and from this angle, instead of a file cabinet, on the platform rested a gargantuan pile of shit, the size of a file cabinet.

"Ugh!" Captain Hart reacted as the smell hit him.

The mass cleared its throat as Hart stepped slightly to the left and saw Grís as the file cabinet again.

"I've been told I have a good side and a bad side," Grís explained.

"Yeah," Captain Hart agreed.

"I think everybody's got that," Captain Boner offered.

"Not like her," Hart countered, looking at his partner with a warning in his eyes.

"Come this way," Grís instructed the captains. "Your birds are molting."

Boner and Hart scooted forward on the platform, glancing over their shoulders. Ichor poured off the surface of the birds, sluicing around the feet of the pilots and off the sides, creating waterfalls of gore that poured into the interior of the edifice. Beneath the ooze, the skin of the birds revealed itself to be volcanic rock, marbled with glowing magma lines, flames blazing from it.

The birds spoke in unison, "We are Hellshrikes. F-666 Hellshrikes."

"O-kaaaaaaaaay." Boner marveled at the transformation. She could feel the heat of the birds washing over her.

When Hart and Boner looked back to Grís they found that the file cabinet had also moved back on the platform. Despite her new form, the consultant did not seem to have an issue getting around.

"Wait, where's General Bowser?" Hart asked. "He's our superior officer, there's no reason we should be reporting to you."

"You report to me now," Grís said grimly. "I'm the one who has the best idea of what we might be dealing with here, and I am not pleased with the way in which I have to live my life at the moment. So I am motivated to do whatever I may need to do to rectify this situation."

"But–" Boner began to object.

Grís cut her off. "The general is off the board. I will say it directly. When the change came, his head was transformed into a hamburger, and as soon as that transpired, the bun ate the patty, leaving him in a vegetative state. It was...a disturbing event for his staff to witness. So now you have me, and it is my intention to resolve the complication, and complete the original objective. We need to stop this extra-planetary incursion as absolutely rapidly as we can. We failed to do so at the Hotel Richmond and everything has gotten much worse. We cannot fail to do so again."

The captains nodded in sharp assent to the statement. Hart swallowed hard, imagining the scene Grís described of General Bowser's unintentional self-mutilation. Hart had worked with the general for years, and felt that they had a mutual sense of purpose for the mission of the SRDF and the sacrifices they were willing to make for that mission. General Bowser had been forced to make the greater sacri-fice, and a terribly grisly one at that.

"All right then," Hart said, hoping to push past this unpleasantness and into a decision about the current plan of action.

"What do we do next?" Boner asked, anticipating Hart's sentiment.

"Next," Grís said, "your law enforcement friends want to debrief you as to what happened on the ground at the Hotel Richmond. There appear to have been additional adver-saries that we had not yet encountered en masse there, and the officers also have information on a couple of new persons of interest. Also, they are puppets now. Your two friends."

"As in, literally?" Boner asked. "At this point, I expect you mean literally."

"Yes, literally. They are literal puppets. Free-standing, free-moving, walk around as they please, children's enter-tainment-style, puppets. To me, that seems like a pretty good bargain," Grís noted. "In any case, your next step is to debrief with the officers, and, armed with that information, to marshal their resources for our endgame.

"For my part, our desire is to find the mastermind, the robot, and neutralize it to prevent further damage and, ideally, reverse the damage done so far. We have a potential resource to help track down where that mastermind may be. I am going to assess and prepare for that. We will rendezvous in the action room, and prepare for our strike against our adversary with all of our assets prepped."

"All right, we need to get to Bunson and Mandel and hear what happened on the ground– wait, what about the unit that was on-site?" Hart asked.

"Apparently the ground vehicles began to shrink rapidly and by all estimations all forces aboard became subatomic within milliseconds and soon thereafter dropped through a hole in the universe to somewhere else."

"Oh..." Boner mumbled.

"You two were lucky. You seem like you are still your-selves, so far," the file cabinet said to the captains, with a lingering note of jealousy. Then it turned, and to *both* Hart and Boner now, it appeared like a ridiculously large pile of shit, gliding away from them, bumping down the stairs leading from the platform and leaving a disgusting streak behind.

57

C heblenkov and Morduar, of the original quintet
that freed Mr. Moon and summoned it to the
Earth, were the only members of the group that
really understood what they were doing.

Dennison was a hedonist, happy to feed his appetites
and do something disgusting to feel richer in deviancy.
Romana understood that it would bring her a new quality of
prominence and power, and fed her hunger to dominate.
Erskine wanted to be scarier.

Cheblenkov and Morduar, however, knew it would
usher in the opportunity to change the way everything
worked. The transformation that they had to endure every
month was chained by so much ungainly structure, so many
rules. They wanted to demolish all of that, no matter the
cost, and make the world a place of unending transformation, unbounded by the prison of substance and time.

And that was why they gathered the others, intimated
that the ritual would change everything, and organized its
execution. It's why Morduar pretended to be so surprised at
returning to his human form as Mr. Moon appeared before

them, appeared to be so horrified when his compatriots fell upon him and tore him to shreds.

But Morduar knew; he knew he would be first, and he knew Cheblenkov would be last. He knew of Cheblenkov's plot to sacrifice one of the pack, and knew it would be him. Morduar willed it when the time came.

Cheblenkov had gathered the others together, and explained to them that a sacrifice would be required, and that they all must agree. Then he told them that they would immediately devour Morduar after they summoned Mr. Moon, and the rest all believed the sacrifice was only Morduar, rather than all of them, together.

Cheblenkov, as a werewolf, had torn Morduar's human head from his neck, and plucked the eyes from the head. The eyes watched from the clearing floor as the rest of his body slithered down the gullets of his compatriots, and Cheblenkov imagined those baby blues were filled with gratitude and happiness to be the first. At least, before Dennison stepped on them and popped them.

Mr. Moon danced and watched it all, and when it was all done, the remaining werewolves, blood-drunk and panting, found the sordid, grinning vision gone.

They went their separate ways into the night, Dennison racing off to find more violence and more meat. Romana loped away, her path separating from Dennison, cutting through the night with the wind on her hide, feeling the power and the promise of the thing. Erskine took a moment, and then followed Romana's trail at a trot, drawn to her and submissive.

Cheblenkov padded around the abyssal circle from which Mr. Moon had emerged, staring into the onyx space within it. And then he took off into the night.

He had spent this time at a cabin near by the mountain,

sitting alone, observing the change in the air as each of the other members of his cadre expired and eroded the gate.

He had felt how the chains of the world cracked and loosened as they slaughtered Morduar, and had then known what to pay attention to as the others met their fate.

Cheblenkov had sat in the cabin's wooden chair, cast over with its worn plaid blanket, as the proportion of magic in every drop of the air had surged.

Now that he was the last, he was ready for a final bit of ceremony, a spectacular ushering in of a new age, unfettered and unrestrained by the old rules of the world. He felt like it needed something auspicious, a small ceremonial act to celebrate this new beginning. He rustled around the pantry of the cabin with a degree of randomness and found an oddly out-of-place decanter: gold, silver, and bronze.

Cheblenkov anointed himself in oil.

And immediately felt entirely disgusting. The sensation on his skin really bothered him, and he didn't understand why anybody would choose to do something like that, especially to feel special.

The oily werewolf, in human form, left the cabin, his shirt collar greasy. He was heading down the mountain, heading to his fate, heading to make sure the new world was the real world for now and ever after.

58

"I'll get it!" Amy called back into the house in response to the doorbell's ring.

"Be careful!" Carol scolded as she joined Amy in the foyer. "I think we should maybe stop answering the door for a while. If it's the trash cans from the alley begging to be fed again, I don't think either one of us will be able to handle it– we should just hunker down, maybe, until this all gets a little more normal."

"Those trash cans were *so* angry," Amy mused, recalling the lids slapping and flopping in agitated complaint at the lack of garbage within. "But for some reason, I have a better feeling about this."

Carol shrugged tightly, unconvinced, and picked up a waist-high ornamental statue that spent its time at the entryway to the entryway.

Amy swung the front door open. "*Biscuit?*" she asked incredulously.

"Hi Amy," Biscuit replied. Then the dog looked past her. "Hi Carol."

Zappazmazoid hovered behind him, studiously looking away from the trio's seemingly intimate moment.

Both Amy and Carol's mouths hung open in surprise. Still, they'd had their trash cans talking to them quite recently, so their prodigal dog doing the same was hardly unthinkable at this point.

"Oh, well, come inside," Amy finally said as their dog looked at them expectantly from the stoop. "And of course your...friend...too. Nice tie, by the way, it suits you."

Biscuit ran his paw down his necktie, smoothing it. "Oh, you think so? Thanks. I just thought I should start dressing the part. You know, since I can talk now."

Zappazmazoid bobbed on the air, following along.

"Come on, let's head to the tv room and catch up," Carol suggested. "I guess if you're walking on two legs and talking, it would be all right for you to get up on the couch for once."

"Well, whatever you're comfortable with," Biscuit said, and settled in on the sofa, legs crossed. Zappazmazoid idled in the air to his right. Carol sat across from them both in a modest chair, drumming her fingers on one knee and studiously looking from side-to-side, rather than directly at either of them.

"Would you care for something to drink?" Amy called, heading to the kitchen. "I think Carol and I could maybe use a little glass of wine. Do you want a little water, in a bowl? Is that what you'd like?"

Biscuit grimaced slightly, and said, "I could have a glass of wine, that sounds nice."

"Ohhhhhhh...kay. Three glasses of white. Oh, your friend, should that be four?" Amy asked.

"I require no wine," replied Zappazmazoid.

"Oh, right, I need to introduce you," Biscuit realized, and waited momentarily, until Amy came back into the room with a small tray on which rested three stemmed wine glasses, each with a generous pour of white wine. She placed the tray on the coffee table in front of the couch, lifted one glass toward Biscuit, and then took one for herself and one for Carol.

As Carol took a strong swallow, Biscuit broke the conversational pause, indicating the levitating robot head with a side flung paw. "This is Zappazmazoid."

"Hello," Zappazmazoid said.

"Pleased to meet you," Amy greeted the robot head. "I'm Amy."

"And I'm Carol," Carol said.

"Hello Amy, Hello Carol," Zappazmazoid said.

"Look," Biscuit began, clearing his throat. "I realize that the way my partnership with Zappazmazoid started was a bit disconcerting, and you both have probably been pretty confused and worried..."

"And I am sorry that I destroyed your shed," Zappazmazoid interjected. "My body had been destroyed, and I could not control the impact velocity of my head."

"Ah. That's okay, we're going to...figure out what to do with the crater. And the debris," Carol replied, sounding unconvinced about that.

"Well, all right. Yeah. We'll figure that out. But we've got, er, bigger bones to gnaw," Biscuit said. "Let me first assure you both that I'm fine, and I've *been* fine, and even though I have the facility to express it now more clearly, that's been the case since square one with my pal here."

Zappazmazoid bounced a bit down and a bit up, conveying an affirmation in a vertical quasi-nod.

"And we're not done yet," Biscuit continued. "There's some danger involved, I'll admit, but I feel like it's more probable I'll have to protect Zappazmazoid than the other way around. We need to finish this business, we need to do it so that things can go back to the way we'd all gotten used to them being, the way we expected them to be. Things have shaken out alright for me..."

Biscuit sipped his wine, and his tongue slopped around his jowls.

"...but I feel like it would be a safe bet that you've seen enough stuff already that it's making you feel a little crazy."

Amy looked meaningfully at Carol, and they both thought of their trash cans, and of the group of birds they saw fly down to their backyard birdbath wearing speedos and carrying a tiny boombox. The music was terrible and the bass shook the china in the cabinet.

"In any case, we're on a mission, and I thought if we had the time, I should actually drop by and keep you both in the loop. I guess I don't want you to worry, but, like I said, it is dangerous and important, so I guess I'm hoping that if you *do* need to worry, it's for the right reasons."

"What is...what...ought...we...worry about?" asked Amy, the words failing her.

"Right, well," Biscuit said. A stout book with *Prisoner of the Moon* printed on its spine was in his lap. Neither Amy nor Carol had noticed it before, or when or how it had shown up there.

"The entity that is responsible for all of this is trying to do some things...some murders...well, exactly one more murder...in order to keep it this way forever. And before that happens, Zappazmazoid needs to capture the entity in this book, in order to send the entity back to the center of the moon, which has been its long-time prison, ever since the time all the living things of the Earth existed in a state of perpetual near-dreaming."

Carol was blinking rapidly at this information, while Amy was not blinking at all.

"Huh." Amy finally processed it enough to drag herself back into the conversation. "Well, I do hope you are as safe as possible. We love you and want you to come back home, and of course if there is any feedback you want to give us while we're able to have the conversation, in brief, we are also open to that. But I imagine this is important enough you need to get right on it, so thank you for taking the time to let us know what you've been up to. Please be safe. Please come home to us. We love you."

Carol opened her mouth, closed it, and then just nodded in assent.

"Oh, we've got a little bit of time," Biscuit confided, draining a bit more of his wine. "We're actually waiting for some things to fall into place, so it was a good time to come by and spend a little time catching up. This thing we're trying to catch, it's not going to poke its head out until the person it's trying to have murdered is at the right place and time, and they're on their way, but not enough to have our thing pop out to get snapped up by the book."

"Okay," Carol said, but didn't really have anything else to add.

Biscuit looked back and forth from Carol to Amy, and back again. "I get it, it's a lot. Why don't we just put something on the tube and enjoy sitting in each other's company."

"That sounds good to me," Zappazmazoid added helpfully.

Carol nodded, then Amy nodded, then Carol reached out for the remote control on the coffee table, flipped on the television, and sat back in her chair.

59

As Grís had informed Hart and Boner, the large domed Secret Rapid Defense Force vehicle from the raid on the Hotel Richmond had shrunk and shrunk and shrunk, so much so that it had eventually slipped between the skin cells laying against the membrane of the smallest scale supported by the universe.

The tactical force within had attempted piloting the vehicle for a short time, but the net effect of that was essentially nil when the direction of motion was a reduction in scale rather than a vector toward a distance. They had taken to mutely observing the cascades of lights and shapes outside the vehicle. Their own surface lights still blinked alternatingly blue and red roughly on the pace of intermittent windshield wipers. As if a pop of red or a blip of blue might clear off the downward journey and reveal that they were just driving along a secluded country road.

There was a point where the disorientation became such that although they were sure they were still shrinking, it felt like they had hit the lowest point on an arc, and were now rebounding back up, like the SRDF vehicle was snapping back, in obedience to some great invisible cosmic bungee cord.

The SRDF agents had the sensation they were rising toward a burgundy plane, and when their vehicle intersected it, they felt that they'd flipped over a gravitational axis and were tumbling back downward. There was a sense of being in interstellar space, but the stars around them moved and seemed to be ornate points from which lines of radiance extended, describing planes of semi-transparent, colored surfaces.

Then, the treaded vehicle toppled to rest against one of the planes, although its surface showed as opaque and was more mottled in texture. Substantial, but soft. The SRDF tank bounced a few times on impact, but didn't suffer any real damage, nor did it cause injury to the ground on which it had landed.

The squad loaded up their armaments once the motion had stopped entirely, and fell into formation. The door of the vehicle slid open on a tap from the squad leader, and they emptied out onto the surface.

"Does the ground seem like it's...a cheap shirt?" Abelhoffer asked, bringing up the rear.

The members of the group that had advanced further had slowed and were looking ahead, rather than down. They seemed to be standing outside what looked like a sleazy roadside motel. But in the future, in space. The SRDF vehicle had come to rest several paces from the motel's office. A bulbous creature stood outside it looking at the agents. It spoke.

"Looking for rooms? We've got the vacancies. Free interstellar entertainment networks between bands fifty and three thousand, with a premium upgrade available to go up to six thousand if you've got the cash to spend. Oh, key deposit is four decicredits. Per key, so that's per room."

Marcy Egg had seen the SRDF descending toward her torso and coming to rest outside the space motel.

It was unusual and high tech enough that it didn't seem out of place in the wide reaches of space, especially considering how peculiar outer space had ended up being. So, Marcy had no thought that its origin was also from the planet Earth. It seemed like it fit in with any of the spacecraft she had seen up to that point, and that it had treads meant for land-bound driving was a little quirk that escaped her notice.

Her two thoughts were:

"That thing looks like a metal egg with a couple red and blue lights stuck on the outside," and "They built this motel in the right place. They didn't even have a grand opening and they're already starting to pack the place out."

The captain started awake when the sound of the SRDF vehicle making impact reached the room as a muffled, bouncy thud. Croax was already standing next to the large window looking out, immediately next to the climate control unit sitting underneath it.

"By heavens, Croax, you're fast!" the captain exclaimed, wiping sweat from his forehead. The room was drenched in heat. He rose from the cheap motel bed, his a-shirt soaked through. "What was that sound? Does it look like trouble?"

Croax parted the blinds with one hand, surreptitiously

removing their other hand from the temperature adjustment panel of the climate control unit. Impassively, Croax replied, "Ribbit."

"All right," the captain agreed, sliding in behind Croax to also get a look. "Right, just looks like other guests, they just had a bit of a rough touch down."

The captain sat back down on his bed, and then groaned. "I. Am. Parched. I have to see if they have a drink machine around here; I need to wet the whistle." He stood and headed to the door, turning back with it cracked half open. "You want anything?"

"Ribbit," replied Croax, declining the offer. As the door closed, the frog person dialed the heat for the room up even further.

Marcy Egg was, at first, not really paying attention when the leader of the travelers from the metal egg ran into the captain of the first group of motel guests at the little vending machine around the corner of the building.

The first captain had been punching buttons on the machine and doing a bit of swearing because the machine was mostly loaded with something that they didn't want, and it was turning out that the one thing they did find palatable seemed to either be sold out or jammed...either way, not dispensing.

The first captain straightened up and engaged the second leader in pleasantries and a bit of artificially amiable conversation when they approached. Marcy was tuned out.

It wasn't as if she were above eavesdropping. She absolutely loved nosing in on the business of the guests of the Royal Leisure Motor Inn while pretending to be absolutely oblivious and disinterested. People were freaks, and getting to witness their freaky little misbehavior, she found fascinating and it also made her feel a little bit superior, which was nice.

But this seemed like boring, empty talk. Or, at least, it did, but it was going on for much longer than she would expect a happenstantial exchange between two strangers at a disappointing vending machine to last.

Marcy Egg's ears perked up when, to her surprise, she realized they were discussing the Earth.

MARCY WAS FEELING AN ANTICIPATORY, stomach-sick excitement, waiting for whatever constituted a full night's stay in space to elapse. The first group's captain and the second group's leader had managed to generate enough of a sense of professional camaraderie around the inadequate vending machine that the former had agreed to tow the latter's vehicle and occupants back to the vicinity of the Earth. A real stroke of luck for the SRDF tactical force.

A real stroke of luck for Marcy Egg, thought Marcy Egg.

When the vehicles blasted off from her surface and began to make their way back through the interstellar void, Marcy was trying to play it cool. Not that any of the guests, or the office manager, would notice. Nobody seemed to pay any mind to the fact that she was, to them, a titanic human woman flung through space as opposed to just a colorful asteroid conveniently situated on a highly trafficked route across the stars.

Still, she didn't want anything to interrupt their plan, which would interrupt her own plan.

As the craft, towing the egg, began to recede, Marcy

began to kick her feet a bit, and commenced to waving her arms to try to slow her momentum in what had been her direction of motion. Like mirrored flagella on either side of her torso, her arms slapped through the ether and began to help rotate her body along an intangible axis running through her hips, in one flank and out the other.

The motel on her body creaked and strained as it was torqued by the action of its host. Inside the office, the office manager clutched the outer corners of their desk madly and yelled   a   tormented   groan,   "PHHHHH-HHNNNNOOOOOOUUUUUR-RRRRRRRGGGGGHHHH!!!!!"

It wasn't an unfamiliar space language, it was just the sound of an office manager being tumbled nauseatingly through the void. It was taking everything the office manager had to hang on and not toss their space cookies or fudge their space trousers.

Marcy Egg, aligned to the trail of the spacecraft and the SRDF tank, began to kick her feet and swing her arms as if breast stroking across the pool of a much nicer motel than either the one at which she worked or the one that was built upon her.

Being a piece of land out in space wasn't too bad, really, but for some reason Marcy Egg really felt like it would be too much giving up, even for her, if she didn't make any kind of effort to get back to Earth with such a convenient opportunity coming to greet her.

60

The Hellshrikes cut a path across the sky, leaving smoke and ash to trace their trails. Captains Boner and Hart could feel the warmth emanating from the giant birds' softly glowing rock flesh, and could smell the brimstone with which they were suffused. Still, they remained unharmed despite being so close to them. It must have been the bond between the pilots and their conveyances that protected the flyers. When the birds eschewed travel by air, flames erupted from the ground at each step, dancing evocatively as the avians walked with languid, high-arched steps.

The captains alit on the roof of the police station and dismounted, the pair of Hellshrikes facing outward over the main entrance; a pair of massive, foreboding crimson-hewed gargoyles temporarily standing sentry over the building.

~

THE DESK SERGEANT, a living portrait composed of vegetables for facial features, nodded and escorted Boner and Hart to the familiar conference room where they had spent time with Bunson and Mandel a short time ago, planning the details of the raid on the Hotel Richmond.

As the sergeant headed back to the desk, Captain Boner realized that she thought he looked a lot like one of the animations she seemed to remember from an old Peter Gabriel video. Maybe it was an image from Sledgehammer, but then again, he went back to the well for Big Time, so maybe it was one of the effects from Big Time. Now an uneven mixture of both songs were going to be sloshing around in her head for a while.

Boner turned her attention to the conference room and followed Hart inside.

There they were, Bunson and Mandel, and they were, indeed, puppets. Nobody acknowledged the change in physicality, and Boner and Hart pulled out their seats across the table from the duo and sat down.

Boner and Hart, unbeknownst to one another, had the same uneasy curiosity and had an invasive urge to drop their heads below the table to see how exactly the puppetry might be working. But, both resisted, and addressed the visible head-arms-torso combos of the officers across from them.

"We've received some intel on what happened on the ground," Hart commenced, "but we lost our squad from the field of engagement, and it is clear we were not successful at forestalling repercussions." He emphasized his point by broadly waving at the puppets to acknowledge the repercussions of which they were very familiar.

Here, Boner took over. "We have an asset that believes we have another opportunity to catch our invader and ideally reverse the effects with which we have had to contend up to this point. But we'd like to hear from you first."

"Invader...about that," Bunson said, his puppet hand lifting to stroke his chin thoughtfully.

"Let's start from the top," Mandel said. "We were aware of the werewolves, we were aware of the robot, we were aware of the werewolves' people. We thought they were just people, maniac people, but it turns out the werewolves had these additional monsters. Nasty cheese people. They didn't need to breathe so our gas didn't have any effect, and whoever was running the show inside the hotel sent them in waves at us."

Bunson nodded, his felt head bouncing up and down.

"So, it was a heavy scrum, and we weren't in position to get into the hotel as a result when the EPMs went in. We saw them launch, and pretty much the moment they went off...well, all this went to hell..." Mandel's wide indication with both arms was accidentally quite showy. "Your big vehicle did the Alice in Wonderland drink-me bit, everybody got a new coat of paint, and the two of us realized somebody needed to get into the hotel and take a survey of the scene right away."

Bunson lifted a hand to pick up the story. If it were articulated enough to do so, his fingers would have spread a wide palm to indicate his intention to carry on the tale. "And this is where it gets particularly interesting, I think. Inside the hotel was a pair of people who were pretty confident they had a better handle on what was going on than we did."

The felt officer began to tap his outstretched hand with his other hand, attempting (and failing) to count off details with his sewn-together fingers. "One, and they were adamant about this, the robot is the one trying to prevent all this from happening. Which means that, two, we're after the wrong suspect and could be spending a lot of resources on the wrong pursuit. That does seem possible and plausible–neither the dog nor the robot were anywhere on sight." Bunson abandoned counting and dropped his puppet hands to the table.

"The werewolves *are* apparently in on all of this, and are part of the plan to make things get weird, but *also* we need to make sure as much as possible that we don't have any more werewolf fatalities, as apparently the unusual stuff happening is directly proportional to werewolf deaths. We had some academics and researchers try to put these pieces together, and they did point us toward a book at a local library that supposedly could explain a lot of this stuff."

"But it was checked out," interjected Mandel.

"Which shouldn't have been possible," Bunson added.

"Because it is a reference book," Mandel said.

"Yep. And it was a little confusing trying to get this out of the librarian, but apparently it was checked out by a dog, and there are different rules for dogs. So mark another tick in the Very Strange Things That Have Happened column," Bunson said.

"So where are these very confident people now?" Captain Boner asked. "It would be good to be able to interrogate them further and try to put these pieces together."

"Agreed," agreed Mandel.

"Unfortunately, they wandered off. It was a pretty chaotic scene, as you can imagine, and, frankly, it still is," Bunson said with an air of defeat, which also happened to be vaguely adorable on account of coming from a puppet.

"I think that sums up the top-level stuff. We should just be very careful. It seems like we've wound up with a real mess on our hands and there are things we do not know that we may need to know to get control of the situation."

"Okay, thank you officers," Captain Boner said. "So, no matter where this ends, we're likely going to see a robot, a dog, a werewolf or werewolves, a pair of people that know some missing pieces of which we are not entirely aware, and possible other unknown actors that need to be controlled or neutralized, who may in fact represent the greatest threat in the whole equation."

"And however it all shakes out," Captain Hart added, "I think we are all going to be happier if all of those individuals are taken off the board."

"So, how do we do it? Where do we think they're all going to be? I don't think they're going to be heading back to the Hotel Richmond," Bunson said.

"Our asset has a resource they believe will guide us to where these interests gather. We're going to rendezvous with them," Captain Hart said. "And I suggest you come with us."

"Sounds good," Mandel said. "The force is spread pretty thin contending with everything the city is throwing at us at the moment, but there's no way you're keeping the two of us out of it. We need to see this through."

Mandel slammed a puppet fist onto the desk in front of them in a very, very cute show of total determination.

61

Dr. Desmond smelled her visitor before she saw her. The doctor had been staring at readouts on a computer screen, elbows on the long desk in front of the bank of displays, hands in her hair at her temples. Her lips had been moving as she struggled fruitlessly to make sense of the details and to shut out the babbling, moaning gibberish resounding from the depths of the laboratory's halls.

As the rank smell overwhelmed her senses, the doctor reeled the swivel chair around to face the entryway of the control center, where she was greeted by a lumpy silhouette framed in the door. She dragged the back of her wrist across her haggard face, and when she opened her eyes again, a file cabinet sat in the middle of the doorway, halfway inside the room.

"Grís," Dr. Desmond seethed with distaste. "I don't have anything to report to you. The drones remain active, they keep talking, they want their queen."

"Martina," Grís replied, her file cabinet form suddenly just a few feet away from the doctor. "Leadership has decided to take a different tack in terms of what we hope to accomplish with your subjects. The constant has been that they seem to want to return to their queen, and given the nature of how things now operate, and the transformation they seem to have achieved, it is believed that, should they be freed from confinement, they will seek out their queen under their own power. There is great interest in locating the queen plant, as it is believed that a related target, one that is most likely responsible for our current operating reality, will also be there. As such, the plants in this facility represent the best resource for leading the appropriate remediation agents to where they need to be."

"You're going to let them out," Dr. Desmond repeated in disbelief. "It's hell to be in here with them, alone, but they're *dangerous*. They've killed, and since then, they've only gotten more dangerous. You're going to be putting people's lives at risk if you just *let them go*. You can't let them out."

"*I'm* not going to let them out, Martina," replied the file cabinet. "You are."

~

DR. DESMOND STOOD in front of the biometric pad next to the giant steel door and shuddered. Rustling noise stirred to a frenzy on the other side, and the cascading sounds of uneven drumming picked up as she looked down at her feet.

"Step aside so I can give the executive sign-off," Grís commanded.

Dr. Desmond grunted an ounce of displeasure and pivoted out of the way. The file cabinet sat for a moment in front of the biometric pad, which somehow managed to register Grís without issue.

"Executive approval: Aemelia Grís, consultant," chimed a digital voice.

Dr. Desmond took a deep breath, then lifted her palm to the pad.

"Scientific approval, Dr. Martina Desmond, chief scientist," chimed the digital voice. "Opening primary vault."

The steel door groaned and began to slide aside. Purple-shaded vegetative tentacles lashed out from within and began to drag their own knotty plant bodies forward. Despite being a population of individual plants, the denizens of the vault advanced as a great, singular wave of biomass; to look into the midst of it revealed separate twisting, looping vines, trunks, and branches swarmed over one another. Each spoke with its own unsettling voice, but, like the physical form emerging from the vault, that manifested as a vile single block of sound.

> *queen i help all i give worm little staggered like to*
> *miss you us our queen through misty keep*
> *queen water take us to the need of our i your*
> *quartet devil is like darkness queen we let's*
> *away fog dancing chilly demand night and*
> *our go and dining queen day haze our queen*
> *room our love queen*

The edges of the mass lashed across Dr. Desmond's feet, and a hard shot knocked her to the ground of the massive aperture. She squeezed her eyes tight, waiting to be dragged into the colony and devoured, but she was left alone, laying on the cold concrete floor. The doctor had been bludgeoned to the ground, and suffered random clubbing lashes in the wake of the collective's motion, but she was not their concern. They desired only to reach their queen.

As the tangled monstrosity squelched its way up the concrete incline to the purple sky of the open air, Dr. Desmond groaned and struggled first to her knees and then to her feet, her ribs screaming in agony. She dragged herself to follow the path of the plants arriving to see Grís, as a pile of shit, already observing their escape. Dr. Desmond drew even to her on the other side of the massive opening to the outside world. When the doctor looked to her left, she again saw the file cabinet. When the doctor looked out, she saw the heap of vegetation crushing its way through the city. A tuna can about the size of an automobile, with car tires on its perimeter, pulled out of an alleyway and began to tail the plants.

High above, a pair of mammoth birds woven with veins of magma across their rocky hides slowly flapped their great wings in order to hover far overhead, also tracing the trail of the drone vegetation on the way to its queen.

Seated on her throne, surrounded by her retinue, the queen shifted and raised her flowering stems into the air, curling and rippling with anticipation.

62

"Thanks for sticking around," Shelly Weedler said to Lazy Nations, who was seated on the couch in Shelly's apartment.

"I suppose I feel a little silly about it, but, shit, I guess I feel like you're one of the only people or things that feels remotely normal to me, and having a little bit of an anchor like that while we deal with all this stuff is helping me relax a little bit. I mean, if you can describe it as relaxing to just be at the point of not totally freaking the fuck out, nonstop."

Lazy Nations nodded in agreement, not adding anything to the sentiment, but not objecting, either.

"Was that an overshare?" Shelly asked self-consciously.

"It's good to have a friend when things are tough. I get you," Lazy said.

"Yeah, that," Shelly agreed, and then dropped into the easy chair. "This is kind of fun, though, too, like a little sleepover situation. Are you sure you're okay on the couch here? If you'd prefer to hop in a bed, you could slip into Gloria's..." She didn't finish the thought, suddenly unsure what was appropriate, what was respectful, and feeling around the outer edge of a lump of sadness she didn't quite understand.

"Nah, couch is fine." Lazy Nations broke the silence. "I like sleeping on couches, that's where I land half the time at my own place. Plus, I don't know, it seems like we should leave your friend's room alone for now. It feels like there needs to be some...closure, I guess. And we're a little too busy thinking about other stuff right now, I bet, for you to be able to get it. So, the couch is great. Couch is great for me."

"OK, super. Thank you for...well, super," Shelly said gratefully. "I don't know if days and nights are things anymore, but it does kind of feel like we've got a chance to sleep a little bit here and treat it like a night. But then again, being awake and not having to deal with crazy shit makes me want to appreciate it a little bit and stretch out. What do you think? Want to watch a little tv?"

Lazy Nations grunted an affirmation, stretched out her legs, and nestled in to watch.

Shelly scooped up the remote control and pressed the power button.

A bright line filled the horizontal space of the screen and then grew to fill the vertical.

ON THE SET, the picture resolved to a strange, opulent processional or receiving line. It looked like a ceremonial arrangement one would expect at the wedding or funeral of someone important, royal, and distant.

There was a red carpet, inlaid with gold, but tattered, stained, and wet in places. After a moment it became apparent that the line was actually outside somewhere– the ambient quality of the purple air was visible in corners of camera shots, and activity far and deep in the sky betrayed the environment. The carpet itself seemed to be stretched across the weathered asphalt of a parking lot.

Bracketing the path of the carpet, a motley array of creatures stood at attention, forming an honorific corridor along its length. An alligator stood on its hind legs, its torso fitted in a tight, double-breasted military jacket adorned with two lines of large brass discs, each row interconnected by another sliver of metal. By its side stood a diseased-looking monkey wearing a monocle over each eye, a chain loosely descending from each lens, connecting to an epaulet on its crushed velvet jacket. Across from them, a tall human skeleton stood, jaw open in a silent scream and pelvis wreathed in unfaltering indigo flame.

The camera tracked along the line and shifted upwards as it followed stair steps to a dais. The periphery of the shot implied that the structure was built on top of a giant, curled human form. Atop the platform was an expansive gilded throne. In it was a majestic, flowing plant, its extremities curling around the throne in places, waving in the air in others; it sat interwoven on top of a pair of human legs– Gloria's legs, Shelly observed– which in turn sat on the throne, elegantly crossed.

The picture reversed angle and swam back down the line, the faces of the eccentric attendees clipping through the borders of the frame. Finally, it broke from the assembly and settled on an approaching figure, heading for the ceremony.

A shot from over the shoulder of the newly arrived individual showed the impressive sweep of the scene. There was, in fact, a giant human curled in an arc, on which towered buildings were cosntructed, with the most visible and impressive edifice being the dais where the queen sat on her throne. The red carpet represented a clear line right to the queen with imposing creatures along either side, but behind them the entire area enclosed by the curled titan was filled with pressing bodies. Plants, animals, monsters (quorbin among them), and humans packed the area straining to see the queen and the path to her.

The camera returned to capture the approach, showing the new arrival: a man bearing an air of menace. He was dressed in worn denim pants, hiking boots, and a threadbare plaid shirt. The collar seemed oddly discolored by a wetness that both darkened it and made it seem almost semi-transparent. The picture lingered on the man's steps down the carpet, the lines of individuals to each side facing him as he passed on his way to the queen.

Then the camera reversed angle again as the man passed through the frame, now following him toward the stairs to the dais. The queen's arms throbbed and waved rhythmically in the air.

As the man achieved the platform, he took several steps toward the throne, then turned and held his arms aloft. The crowd cheered, a mismatched cacophony of sounds made by a vastly diverse array of voices. The man dropped his arms to his sides, and leaned slightly backward as tentacles from the queen snaked out, entwining themselves around the man, squeezing him tightly, and lifting him into the air as a totem for all below to see. The congregation erupted again.

Behind the throne, the moon hung in the purple sky, full and shining.

～

SHELLY CLICKED OFF THE TELEVISION. She and Lazy sat up in their seats, spines straight, eyes wide and staring at the blanked screen.

"That wasn't a show," Lazy said.

"Nope. No it wasn't. Shit. That...my television just showed us something that is happening someplace? Has happened? Is about to happen? Fucker. That...that ..." Shelly stammered as images of what she'd seen flickered through her mind.

"That was our last werewolf, the guy in the vines," Lazy said. "We've got to get to him before they kill him. They're going to kill him and seal the deal."

"That's not all," Shelly said. "I mean, that is all. That's the whole thing, nothing else matters aside from keeping that fucker alive until Biscuit and Zappazmazoid can catch the thing, and then, y'know, fuck that guy, then. I need to call Zappazmazoid and let him know this is going on. Maybe he knows. BUT. But, also worth noting, I guess. The, um, royal plant– the queen– it has Gloria's legs. It's wearing her skirt and boots too. AND, I've seen that plant before. A guy drove it out of the place across the street right before all this shit started happening. And not just *any* guy. Oh no, I mean, shit. The big guy...the, the person that has all the buildings built on them. That's the guy that drove the plant away from the place across the street. So. So, I guess he got fucked. Right?"

"Yes," Lazy agreed slowly. "But I don't think that changes anything. We've got to go and grab that werewolf, and keep him alive until Zappazmazoid does his thing."

"Sure," Shelly said. "But go where? Did you recognize where that was? I've seen the guy before, but I've never seen him that big. Or, you know, as a building."

"Yeah, yeah, I did recognize it," Lazy Nations said. "I saw

a sign in one of those wide shots. It's the Royal Leisure Motor Inn."

"The what?" Shelly asked.

"The Royal...it's a sleazy no-tell motel type place on a service road off the highway. It's gross," Lazy Nations explained.

"All right, then, let's go," Shelly said enthusiastically. "We've got to save the world! Or at least save the werewolf, and let Zappazmazoid save the world. Sleepover is over!"

Marcy Egg had been breast stroking across the distance of the interstellar void, following the spacecraft and the SRDF vehicle it was towing.

She had never been overly obsessed with the idea of space or the planets or any of that science-y type stuff, but she was still able to recognize Saturn off to her right and realize that they were getting close.

It was after she picked her way through the asteroid belt that another human figure caught her eye.

That's weird. How many of us are out here floating around in dang...space, these days?

The figure was frozen, literally frozen, with an expression of eyebrow-raised surprise on his face. He was dressed like a hiker, one arm raised above his head.

Marcy was not, by nature, a particularly generous or considerate person, which she thought helped her do her job behind the desk at the Royal Leisure Motor Inn. But, perhaps because she had faced the prospect herself recently, the idea of abandoning another person to float forever through the empty soup of space felt actively cruel. Her typical approach was more one of passive impassivity, and ignoring the plight of this castaway would feel like a willful act of violence against him.

It meant she would fall slightly behind the pace of the spacecraft and its SRDF charge, but she was close enough to home that she felt like she didn't need to trail them so tightly anymore. Marcy Egg scooted over to the frozen hiker, grabbed a brittle boot string in one fist, and kicked off an asteroid to power herself Earthward.

Almost home.

64

B eautific Nations poured himself a drink, and ambled inside his living room, still creaking and popping from having been recently tossed around. He wasn't a young man anymore, and it was taking him a little bit of time to work out the kinks and hitches suffered at the hands of his monstrous neighbor.

His living room wasn't in much better shape. The coffee table had been returned to its upright position, but the room was still in some disarray, and the dings in the walls were obvious reminders of the dust-up.

In addition to all that, a flickering sense of unease had been accompanying Beautific's physical discomfort. Lazy had called him a couple of times to check in, but she'd been a bit terse in describing the overall picture and what precisely she was up to. She was handling it, he had been assured.

Still, the one thing that Beautific knew was that his daughter knew how to kick ass, better than anybody he had ever met, known, or heard about. If it came down to it, and something needed its ass kicked to get everything back in shape, Lazy was going to be the one that could do it.

Beautific was concerned about his kids, but not really worried. They'd turned out great, probably in spite of his unconventional approach to raising them, and he trusted them, and he loved them.

He took a sip and sat in the quiet. This was a new, odd feeling. He had no doubt that his daughter would do whatever she needed to do, but he couldn't help being anxious about her having to go through it.

65

E ven from a distance, it wasn't difficult to see where the activity was. And once Shelly Weedler and Lazy Nations drew close to the transfigured Royal Leisure Motor Inn, it wasn't difficult for them to blend in to the throng radiating out from it.

At the periphery, the crowd was mostly human beings, standing, dazed and wobbling in place, eyes directed toward the motel. They had begun to gather as far back as the highway, lining the exit ramp down to the service road, the collection of people and things growing thicker at the service road and forming concentric rings across parking lots and sidewalks and under the highway, with the motel as the hub of the gathering.

Shelly and Lazy pushed past the bodies and headed toward the motel, the bizarre sight they'd seen on Shelly's television appearing before them as they got closer and closer to the center point. The nearer they got, the stranger the attendees to the ceremony became: fewer humans, more animals and objects (mostly standing and dressing like humans), and more quorbins. By the time they'd managed to settle in close to the red carpet, they were packed tight, shoulder-to-shoulder with a completely heterogeneous collection of celebrants. The fact that they were both human, and next to each other, could have drawn attention as something rather unusual given the surrounding population. But everyone and everything was exultantly glued to the werewolf, still in human form, held aloft by several of the snaked arms of the seated plant queen. The air filled with staccato indecipherable chatter, over which a musical hum emanated.

As Shelly and Lazy looked around, trying to get the lay of the land and formulate a plan for surmounting the sea of adversaries, there was a shift. The sound of the crowd began to coalesce into something that felt like a fanfare composed of all the disparate voices of those gathered. The air became thicker, heavier, and warmer, and the saturation of the already lush sky deepened. The crowd followed the attention of the werewolf and the queen down the red carpet, past its terminal point, and off in the direction the werewolf had emerged from earlier.

A dancing figure was approaching, its elbows swinging up and legs kicking out here and there as it advanced. It occasionally snapped its fingers, drummed them across its chest, or slapped its hands together.

It was huge, much bigger than a human being, like a grotesque fast food mascot brought to life. The creature was possibly ten feet tall, and took up nearly as much space around it, due to the size of its giant spherical head. It wore a double-breasted suit which flashed silver as it danced, and a comparatively tiny matching fedora, cockily slung back on the orb of its head. That head was a caricature of the moon, illuminated by a glow from within and pockmarked here and there by craters. Its eyes were both vacant and soulshakingly malevolent, rapacious and greedy above a massive grin that stretched nearly from one side of the sphere to the other.

Shelly heard Lazy beside her, cracking her knuckles once again, and she marveled at her friend's complete acceptance of the possibility of putting herself in the path of a seemingly unwinnable challenge.

As Mr. Moon drew nearer, a human being in the crowd leapt up with an outstretched hand, and without breaking its shuffling steps, it high-fived the offered hand. The human's body immediately washed away as if it were liquid, leaving a skeleton frozen in the position of the leaping high-five. The skeleton exploded into dust and dispersed on the wind.

There was an intake of breath as Mr. Moon continued to dance forward, and then the whole assembly cheered. The crowd flowed toward the prancing entity in waves, desperate for contact, and Mr. Moon easily incorporated more high-fives into the steps of its advance. Recipients sluiced away, and Mr. Moon was haloed in a cloud of bone dust. Every so often, the effect of making contact yielded a different result. A three-and-a-half foot tall rat wearing a basketball jersey and backwards cap disassembled into a cluster of fireworks that blazed across the sky, raining sparks down below. A woman in a long ball gown collapsed into a quivering ball of fleshy mess which pulsated on the path behind Mr. Moon, from time-to-time launching a plume of gore into the air timed to the dissolution of subsequent revelers.

Lazy Nations was rolling her shoulders a bit to loosen up and create some space, subtly moving herself and Shelly closer to the red carpet and the dais, when Mr. Moon arrived at the furthest edge of the carpet, by now buffeted by a wall of billowing skeletal debris.

Mr. Moon paused, its eyes falling upon its servant and final obstacle to fully governing the nature of reality. Cheblenkov was lifted higher and higher by the arms of the queen. The werewolf closed his eyes and lifted his face in supplication. Impossible though it may have appeared, Mr. Moon's grin seemed to grow wider.

BUNSON AND MANDEL'S tuna can car sped after the tangled mass of drone plants crushing its way through the city blocks. Above, Captains Boner and Hart kept pace upon their Hellshrikes.

"It's heading for the highway," Mandel noted as the cluster of vegetation shifted its course toward an onramp, crushing any automobiles parked along the street. The tuna can car tried admirably to keep up.

"Look out, it's taking the next exit already," Captain Boner reported down to Bunson and Mandel. "But I think you're going to have trouble on the ground. It looks as though there's an accumulation of on-foot individuals choking the area, starting at the top of the exit and getting denser from there. Get as far as you can, but you may have to continue on foot."

The captains stayed in pursuit of the botanical behemoth, watching as it plowed through anything in its path. As it moved, the crowd simply reformed in its wake, without notice or concern for those mashed into a pulp by the migrating mass.

Meanwhile, Bunson and Mandel's tuna can car slowly navigated through the crowd, its horn and siren blasting dolphin songs. Virtually ignored by the pedestrians around it, they finally gave up near the top of the off-ramp. The pull tab popped up, the lid on the top of the car peeled back, and the two puppets crawled over the lip of the can onto the street. Bunson double-clicked the lock button on his key fob, and the lid rolled itself back straight to cover the contents of the car, pushing a poof of tuna smell out onto the street. The pull tab dropped back down, and the puppets turned to bounce-run their way down the exit ramp to follow the trajectory of their air bound companions.

Each held a comically large service weapon in their felt hands.

"WHERE THE FUCK IS ZAPPAZMAZOID?" Shelly asked through her teeth. Mr. Moon had grooved its way all the way to the steps of the dais, past the honor guard arranged on each side of the red carpet.

"I don't know, but we can't wait," Lazy Nations replied as she began shoving her way through the crowd. "I'm going to have to buy the robot some time by kicking this thing's ass."

"Shit," Shelly declared.

Mr. Moon turned again to face the crowd. It began pumping its pelvis to the rhythm of the moment. Pump. pump. pump. On the beat, Mr. Moon produced a tiny silver pistol.

Mr. Moon's head swiveled back and forth, giving everyone within the arc of the Royal Leisure Motor Inn a view of its demonic grin. Framing it from behind, every limb of the queen plant currently *not* knotted around Cheblenkov waved ecstatically.

The crowd simmered down in anticipation as Mr. Moon turned again toward the dais and trilled its feet up the steps, barely kissing each one with the tip of a leather loafer.

Standing in front of Cheblenkov, Mr. Moon gripped the silver pistol in both hands over its head and lowered its straight arms in a smooth arc so that it pointed directly into Cheblenkov's face.

Mr. Moon squeezed the trigger.

A shot rang out.

It did not find its mark.

Mr. Moon had been shoved from behind.

The silver bullet merely grazed Cheblenkov's skull, and the werewolf began to die, but it would be a slow, prolonged death as the hint of silver now needed time to take fatal hold across his body. This was especially true because of the nature of reality. Waves prefer drama to simple cause and effect, and that meant Cheblenkov would be passing from the world through a long, vibrating tunnel, rather than in an abrupt burst.

Mr. Moon spun angrily to see who had dared to lay hands on it. Shelly Weedler stood there on the top stair of the dais, her hands still open and braced in front of her. Several steps down, Lazy Nations looked up at her, stunned. Lazy had cleared the crowd and broken through the honor guard in a series of blows, grapples, and throws, while Shelly had taken the opportunity to slip underneath the brawling and run up the stairs to interrupt Mr. Moon's attempt at ceremonial murder.

Mr. Moon's teeth parted to reveal an endless black abyss within its cranium, and it screamed a scream of rage that defied sound, ripping across everyone like a concussive blast. Shelly's knees buckled, Lazy raised her arms and braced herself in a crouch, the queen's vine-y arms shrank back in horror, and much of the crowd fell partially, if not completely, to the ground.

Mr. Moon slapped Shelly, and she left her feet, hurtling

end-over-end and landing painfully on the dais. Mr. Moon repeated its ceremonial motion, lifting its hands over head and pointing the silver pistol directly into the face of the gray and withering Cheblenkov. This time it moved quickly, going through the motions, but with none of the bravado and flair packed into the first attempt. Lazy Nations sprang forward, rushing up the stairs to follow Shelly's lead and stop the murder.

"Selene!" a voice cried from the red carpet, the corners of the words buzzing with frayed digital sparks.

Everyone froze in place. Zappazmazoid hovered over Biscuit's left shoulder, addressing the infernal entity on the dais. Biscuit, standing on his hind legs, held open the book *Prisoner of the Moon*, neatly at the midpoint. Across both pages was the drawing of a great elliptical shape, impossibly black and disorienting in its depth.

"It is time for you to return to your confinement, this world is not for your kind," Zappazmazoid declared.

The ellipse on the book began to inhale, and Mr. Moon tumbled toward it. Lazy Nations could feel the sensation of pulling and the disorientation was severe, but it seemed that the trap printed in the book was exclusively meant to draw in Mr. Moon. Everyone else could only feel its pull as an immutable opinion on what it thought the rules of reality ought to be.

Mr. Moon stumbled toward the ellipse, and though the monster was giant, it seemed, also, to be just small enough to slide into the pages of a book.

～

CAPTAINS BONER and Hart felt certain they were closing in on whatever was responsible for the damage to the integrity of the world. They both knew that wherever the giant mobile garden was heading was where they would find the source of the problem, whether it was their extra-planetary robot head, its dog, some other plant thing, a cheese monster, or something else entirely. They felt, with the instincts honed by years of sorties, that the conclusion was drawing nigh.

So it came as a surprise to find themselves caught in a trap. By the time their Hellshrikes swooped toward the crucible of the Royal Leisure Motor Inn, the plants they'd pursued there had already rooted themselves as a giant impassable wall between them and the motel.

The captains drew their bird mounts up hard, but great swatting stalks and grasping vines threw themselves toward the captains, forcing them to bank away. They reoriented and directed their Hellshrikes to spout flame toward the vegetation, but more plants rose to replace those reduced to ash.

Captain Boner flew in, much *too* close it turned out, and with a fierce jolt, a spiked tendril pierced the side of her Hellshrike, the impaled bird shuddering and dying beneath her, still pinned up by the brutal vine. As Boner turned, waving to Captain Hart to retrieve her, she watched in horror as he was bludgeoned off his Hellshrike, his broken body spinning down and into the clutching nightmare of the vegetation below.

"Rick!" Boner shouted helplessly, knowing it was already too late for him. Her only option now was to save herself. She leapt from the corpse of her Hellshrike to plummet through the air onto the back of Hart's abandoned bird. She pulled hard against it and withdrew from the vicious swarm of attacks, looking to recalculate an approach and putting the death of her partner, for the moment, out of her mind.

ZAPPAZMAZOID WATCHED IMPASSIVELY as Mr. Moon fought to escape the ellipse at the center of the *Prisoner of the Moon*, still held carefully aloft by Biscuit.

The monster braced each of its patent leather loafers against the sliver of blank page on either side of the ellipse, leaning back away from it in an effort to remain free. On the dais, the color ebbed from Cheblenkov's skin. If Mr. Moon could remain free until the werewolf was gone, matter would wave forevermore.

There was a palpable stillness to the moment. It felt like it was going on forever with little real motion. Lazy Nations stepped back down the stairs to observe the scene. There was the robot head, hovering as the arbiter of the moment. The dog, holding open the book. The fantastic creature, struggling against being absorbed. The surrounding, fallen crowd, trying to lift itself back up like background figures in some old oil painting.

She gazed up, past the struggle, and realized there had risen a giant, throbbing wall of flora on the outskirts of the crowd. It seemed to sequester the Royal Leisure Motor Inn from the rest of the world; they were alone now, on this anvil where the rules of how things work would be crafted, one way or another. Lazy spared a glance back to the dais, and saw that Shelly was moving, painfully lifting herself to her hands and knees from where she had been thrown.

Then, motion returned to an expected speed, horribly.

Mr. Moon pointed its silver pistol between its knees and pulled the trigger. Rather than discharging a silver bullet, it flared, as if it were a novelty cigarette lighter. The flame from its barrel engulfed the book– and *Prisoner of the Moon* burned. The black ellipse curled, along with the other pages, to ash gray in fractions of a second, the spine of the book crumbling inward.

"No!" cried Zappazmazoid.

Too late, the robot discharged a laser from its head toward the silver pistol. At the same moment, Mr. Moon swung the pistol toward the floating robot head and pulled the trigger again. The pistol and Zappazmazoid exploded together, showering the carpet in mixed fragments of metal.

"Zappazmazoid!" cried Biscuit.

Mr. Moon kicked the dog, and the chocolate lab flew through the air in a high arc, landing in the crowd beyond with a wounded yelp.

"All right, that's enough," Lazy Nations said firmly, fully aware that this might be her last fight.

Mr. Moon turned back toward Lazy Nations, grinning wide. She was the only thing between him and the throne.

CAPTAIN BONER LOOPED in the air, maintaining a safe distance from the wall of violence imposed by the drone plants. She tracked the motion of the thrashing tendrils, seeing no way to fly through the flailing chaos in the sky.

Fine. She wouldn't go through. She would go *under*.

Boner swooped her Hellshrike to the ground, pushing pedestrians away in every direction. Once its feet had touched down, she urged it forward, and the giant smoldering bird began to sprint past the foliage wall and toward the Royal Leisure Motor Inn.

LAZY NATIONS and Mr. Moon ran toward each other. A few steps before they met, Lazy clasped her hands together, leapt, and managed to land a downward chop, Captain Kirk-style, in a double fist hammer blow.

Surprised, the bludgeoned thing landed on one knee, flailing its arms in little circles to not fall backwards. For just a moment, the wide grin popped to a small surprised circle. But there was no celebrating this small victory. Mr. Moon's servants quickly rose in a looming crest above her, and Lazy prepared to be mobbed by the collection of adversaries. An alligator in a brass-buckled double-breasted military jacket opened its jaws wide.

Toby Chompers, though, was the first to fall. The alligator took a comically large bullet through the eye, the back of his skull shattering from the exit wound, as the puppets Bunson and Mandel bounced down the red carpet, their weapons swinging around for targets among the creatures crowding inward.

"This is the guy!" yelled Lazy Nations. "Keep all these other things off of me, I'm going to kick this thing's ass!"

Bunson and Mandel's puppet heads bounced in acknowledgment and broke out to keep a circle of protection around the pugilists' encounter, firing off a bullet every time one of the assailants got too close. They felled a skeleton with a blazing pelvis, followed immediately by a rolled up Persian rug adorned with googly eyes.

Lazy, meanwhile, landed a one-two combination against Mr. Moon's giant head and it jerked back from the impact. It almost didn't seem fair, considering that it was such a huge target. Mr. Moon jumped back and raised its fists, hopping back and forth from foot to foot, and dipping the globe of its head to one side, cocking up to land blows of its own.

Unrattled, Lazy moved in, poised in a similar boxer's

stance and looking to press her advantage. At once, both combatants shifted unexpectedly, kicking each other in the groin in unison. Both Lazy Nations and Mr. Moon doubled over, bent forward and breathing hard to push the gut twisting pain down.

Bunson and Mandel were now struggling at the surge of adversaries pushing in on them, and their defensive perimeter seemed doomed. Then, to everyone's surprise, a rumpled monkey dramatically leaping toward Mandel's back was caught mid-air in the mouth of a huge rocky bird that had cut its way through the gathered bodies. The monkey was flash-fried by a burst of heat from Captain Boner's Hellshrike and swallowed whole. The bird breathed a spray of fire and pushed back the attackers coming in at them. Captain Boner leapt from the bird's back and joined the fray. From out of the crowd, Biscuit appeared, limping but ready to fight. The dog had retrieved a flagpole from somewhere, and was using it like a bo staff to knock back enemies and sweep creatures off their feet.

Reinforcements were nice, Lazy Nations thought, as the pain in her guts eased. But, watching Mr. Moon recover at the same rate, she realized this was a losing fight. The book that could trap the creature was gone, and as soon as the last pillar of the gate finished dying, that was the end of it. The world would be Mr. Moon's.

Except. The last pillar of the gate. The gate. It wasn't entirely gone.

Lazy surprised Mr. Moon with a quick scissor kick to its trunk, and then punched downward onto its skull with each fist.

"Shelly!" she yelled up to her friend on the dais, where Shelly was still struggling to push herself entirely to her feet. "The werewolf! The werewolf is the last piece of the gate! We have to get this thing through the gate before the werewolf dies! Get him free of those vines!"

Shelly nodded, despite gravity pulling at her unreasonably, and then forced herself forward, limping and lurching over to the dying werewolf. She tore at the vegetation wrapped around him, shredding it as it fought against her. The queen's free arms grabbed at Shelly's feet, flipping her onto her back, and dragging her away from Cheblenkov.

Below the dais, on the carpet, the puppets, the captain, the dog, and the Hellshrike battled fiercely. Lazy Nations took a few glancing shots from Mr. Moon, but was dominating the creature, landing body blows with her hands, elbows, and knees. It was desperate, though, because when Cheblenkov died, it was all over. That Lazy Nations seemed built to kick ass, any ass at all, probably wasn't going to matter when what she was trying to fight was the governor of all reality. This was rope-a-dope on a cosmic scale.

Once she'd been pulled into the heart of the queen's foliage, the viscous greenery began to choke and smother Shelly. Already hurt, she felt her vision blur around the edges as she struggled desperately to fight off the vines. Color popped in bursts against a blackening vision of the queen.

At that precise moment, a giant crash rang out across the valley of the service road where the Royal Leisure Motor Inn lay nestled. A huge, domed vehicle, shaped roughly like a massive metal egg and blinking with alternating red and blue lights, had dropped from the heavens and crushed a large section of the massive wall of plants. The egg teetered briefly, and then began rolling forward out of the wreckage.

The queen screamed, its psychic children mutilated beyond repair by the SRDF vehicle returning to Earth. Shelly's vision cleared enough for her to resume fighting:

she braced her feet against the hips of Gloria's legs, wrapped her arms around the trunk of the queen, and shoved with all her might, straining to straighten her body and rip upwards.

The queen screamed again, and tore from Gloria's legs, viscera neither animal nor plant jaggedly separated from each side of the composite body. Shelly tried not to vomit as Gloria's legs kicked wildly on the throne, and the queen's vegetative body did the same.

Pushing past her revulsion, Shelly scrambled back to Cheblenkov's prone form, and began tearing the foliage wrappings from the werewolf's graying body. His breath was shallow and rattling.

"Lazy! I've got him!" Shelly called, her breath jagged, her body bruised.

"Great, we've got to get this piece of shit inside him!" Lazy called back. She'd managed to wrap an arm around Mr. Moon's neck, and was repeatedly punching the creature directly in the face, hard. Mr. Moon had gone limp, although its eyes were wide and it continued to smile broadly. The tips of its shoes dragged across the carpet as Lazy dragged him up the steps.

"Inside...?" Shelly tried to understand.

Cheblenkov's eyes fluttered. He was nearly gone, but slipped into consciousness enough to distantly perceive what was happening. The werewolf locked his jaw closed with all the force left in his body.

"The werewolf is the last part of the gate, we should be able to get this thing back through the gate it came through in the first place! Before the gate is gone!"

"He's got his mouth closed really hard!" Shelly yelled back, scrabbling her fingers at the corners of Cheblenkov's mouth and trying to wiggle them inside in an attempt to pull his jaw apart.

"Get his pants, his pants!" Lazy hoarsely returned. Mr. Moon spun its arms on each side in an attempt to free itself from Lazy's iron hold.

"Oh boy," Shelly said, hustling to roll Cheblenkov over onto his belly as his eyes popped wide. She jerked Cheblenkov's worn denim jeans down to his knees, exposing his bare bottom to the circus of carnage.

"Here we go," Lazy declared as she reached the top of the dais. She slapped Mr. Moon's stupid fedora off its head with one hand, and then jammed the sphere of its head against Cheblenkov's ass, starting to push hard.

Mr. Moon started to slide into Cheblenkov, shrinking as it tried, in vain, to wiggle free. After several vigorous pushes, its whole upper body was in Cheblenkov's asshole, hands pinned to its hips, slapping away. Its legs pumped as if it was riding a bicycle. Then Lazy gave one more hard push to the soles of its shoes, and the entirety of Mr. Moon disappeared into the last remaining fragment of the gate, Cheblenkov.

For his part, Cheblenkov experienced a massive, massive orgasm. And then died.

EVERYTHING BECAME NORMAL, immediately.

More or less.

Everyone that had become something other than human, became human again. Everything that wasn't human, but started acting that way, reverted to its inert state. So the area around the service road was filled with massive crowds of very confused people and a whole lot of garbage.

The Royal Leisure Motor Inn returned to its previous structure, albeit even dirtier and with ruined ceilings and walls radiating from number six. The hole to the sewer was visible in the room through the gaping holes in the walls, and it mostly didn't have a roof.

Wyatt, the lab assistant, lay in the position he'd assumed when he served as the motel itself, crying quietly with his eyes pressed closed.

Bunson and Mandel were human again, and stood in the parking lot, trying to shake themselves into feeling normal. Captain Boner stood with them, and a fighter jet blocked the service road, its nose cone positioned above the group.

Shelly and Lazy, bruised and exhausted, stood a few paces away, near the door to number six. At their feet was Cheblenkov's corpse, withering away.

The sky had returned to its normal blue-black night hue, and the moon gleamed full in it.

Biscuit ran up to Shelly and Lazy, tongue hanging out and favoring one foot a bit.

"Oh, good boy," Shelly greeted him. "I guess it's going to be hard for you to tell us where your home is now, huh. It was easier when you could say stuff."

"Oh, I can tell you where I live, no problem," Biscuit replied.

Lazy and Shelly's jaws fell open in tandem, truly surprised.

"Yeah, I know," Biscuit said. "Reality is kind of like the neck of a t-shirt, you know. Once it gets stretched out, it's always going to be a little bit loose in places. You can't put it back. Is that a decent description? I am a dog."

Marcy Egg and Joe Hickock gently floated down into the parking lot of the Royal Leisure Motel Inn, their feet coming to a rest on the asphalt in a slow roll.

Marcy looked around the parking lot flatly. The place was well and truly trashed.

"W-w-w-hat happened?" Joe Hickock asked, teeth chattering, arms wrapped around himself. "W-w-w-here am I?"

Marcy Egg sighed deeply.

"The Royal Leisure Motor Inn," she finally replied, turning to walk toward the office. "I think we'll have a vacancy if you need a room. But it's a five dollar key deposit.

"Cash only."

ACKNOWLEDGMENTS

I wrote Lunacy in November of 2023, finally taking a shot at the fifty thousand word novel writing challenge for the month. I wrote just over fifty thousand words, then I stopped working on it, and Mary Winn has done all of the work since then. She's the best, I love her, and am really lucky she loves me.

Let's get the fact I'm going to forget someone(s) or something(s) really important out of the way right at the start here. In fact, let me leave some white space so we can write it into your copy so it's out there somewhere:

My father made sure that reading was a part of every night of my childhood, and that will be a highlight of my whole life. I wonder how he's going to feel about this. Maybe as flustered and angry as he got when we wouldn't let him get away with skipping the levitating sex scene in So Long, and Thanks for All the Fish.

Apologies to my mom for being really critical of the short story she wrote when I was in high school about the person swimming in the hotel pool. Writing is hard, and I was a real turd about her foray into it.

Particular thanks to Nick, Louie, and Nathan for reading and commenting on the original document. The interest and participation and feedback were very heartening. Matt, Jacob, and Gus put eyes on it too, and those conversations made me happy. I wish I could find the exact quote Jim had, because I wanted to use it as a blurb, but it's lost to the sands of time. It was something like "What if Stephen King was hornier?!"

And thanks to the crew keeping it going in November 2024: Nick (again) and Emily especially because they managed to make it over fifty thousand words. But also Andrew, Anthony, Keller, and Lydia for giving it a shot. It's plunging oneself into a maniacal place to do this kind of thing in that kind of timebox. But, let's see, my 2024 sword-and-sorcery effort *The Legend of the Rainbow Blades* may make it into your hands at some point, and we'll see what happens in 2025.

It was a profoundly determinative event for me to fall into improv thanks to my parents and my pal Jim when I was turning seventeen. Turns out it really fits me. I have tried across my life to write various things, but I just didn't have the tooling for it. Then, here, I took the techniques from week three of the improv class I teach in the curriculum at CIC theater in Chicago, and wrote stuff down instead of putting it on a stage. I'm surprised it worked in a way other attempts haven't. That was a pretty cool discovery.

I've got a lot of gratitude for all of the teams, theaters, teachers, coaches, and individuals with whom I've crossed paths. The long-standing ones especially: Rainbow Deli, Revolver, Mustang Repair, Pudding-Thank-You, and the Princeton New Money @$$ Clowns.

I'm a huge fan of a lot of things. Here are three:

Daniel Pinkwater
    The Firesign Theatre
    SCTV

Thanks for taking the time with this, and I hope we both have in front of us more things that make life great than make life tough!

ABOUT THE AUTHOR

Jorin Garguilo is an improviser based in Chicago. This is Jorin's first novel.

www.ingramcontent.com/pod-product-compliance
Lightning Source LLC
Chambersburg PA
CBHW020135120726
47903CB00007B/2271